The Tattoo Collector

Also by D.H. Jonathan:

The "Volunteer"
Life Models
The Girl Who Stopped Wearing Clothes

The Tattoo Collector

D. H. Jonathan

Naturale Publishing

2024

For my brothers Garon and Brian.

1

When Donald White saw the murdered girl's photo on the news website, his already waning motivation for work disappeared. She looked exactly like the girl from his last nightmare about a month before, one of a series of nightmares that were more like visions and that had plagued him on and off for the last fifteen years. The photo appeared to be a high school yearbook picture of an eighteen-year-old brunette. She wore glasses, the frames black with green highlights in the corners. The girl in his nightmare had worn identical glasses. The girl in his nightmare had also had a small scar that split her left eyebrow, identical to the scar on the girl in the photo.

Donald had only just sat down and logged into his computer. The first thing he checked each morning was Outlook, but on this particular morning, he had seen nothing in his Inbox that required his immediate attention, so he opened his web browser. The default home page, which he had never bothered to change in the two and a half years he had been working here, was an MSN news site that included a section for local and regional stories. It was the photo that captured his attention more than the headline, "Police identify body of young woman found at Holland Lake Park."

The young woman in the photo was Elena Robles from Saginaw, Texas. The story described how her parents had reported her missing after she had failed to return home from a Saturday night graduation party in the stockyards area of

Fort Worth. Two of her best friends said that she had left the party at about 12:30 AM in her black Hyundai Accent. That Hyundai had been found abandoned on the shoulder of Interstate 30 near the Ridgmar Mall in west Fort Worth the following morning, its front left tire flat.

Donald's mouse cursor was jumping all over the screen, and he realized that he was trembling. He took his hand off the mouse and took a deep breath as he continued reading. Elena had remained missing for three weeks despite televised pleas from her parents and siblings. A partly decomposed body had been found two days ago at Holland Lake Park in Weatherford, about thirty miles west of Fort Worth, and that body had recently been identified as Elena Robles's.

Donald pushed himself away from his desk and stood up.

"You all right?" Jeff asked from the cubicle next to his.

Donald looked at Jeff without saying anything and started walking toward the elevators.

"Don, what's wrong?" Jeff asked, but Donald kept walking.

His stomach cramped up before he got to the elevators, so he turned and made a beeline for the men's room. He just made it into the stall and bent over the commode before the breakfast burrito he had eaten on the drive to the office shot up and out along with whatever else had been in his stomach. Once he had retched what he hoped was his last, he flushed and exited the stall. He was bent over the sink rinsing his mouth when Jeff walked in.

"Shit," he said, waving his hand in front of his face as if to push the stench away. "Are you OK?"

"Yeah," Donald replied. "Breakfast didn't agree with me, apparently."

Jeff made use of the urinal, but his gaze remained on Donald. "You still look pretty pale."

"Yeah. I think I'm gonna take the rest of the day off."

Donald wiped his face with a paper towel, wishing he had a toothbrush and toothpaste at his desk. Or at least a bottle of mouthwash. He took a look at himself in the mirror, noting how pale his normally tanned face looked. His dark brown hair was unkempt, and he tried to brush it back with his fingers.

"You gotta take care of yourself," Jeff said.

"Yeah." Donald, still feeling queasy, walked out of the restroom and to his manager's office.

"Hey Vanessa," he said from her open door.

Vanessa, blonde hair pushed back into a ponytail, was nearing fifty but still looked to be in her thirties. She had never married as far as anyone knew because she never talked about her personal life at the office. Jeff had mused aloud to Donald on more than one occasion whether she might be batting for the other team, not that it mattered much to Donald since he was happily married. Vanessa looked up from her screen, and Donald could register the change of her expression to one of mild shock. "Hey, what's up?"

"I'm not feeling so well. I mean, I know I just got here, but something hit me all of the sudden."

"Yeah, you don't look well," Vanessa said.

"I think I'm going to turn around and use a PTO day. If that's OK."

"Yeah sure," Vanessa said. "Do you have anything outstanding right now?"

"Just a couple of new phone configurations. I'll send those tickets to Jeff." Donald was transferring them on the ticketing app on his phone even as he spoke to Vanessa.

"All right. Get to feeling better."

"Thanks."

Donald stopped by his cubicle to get his regular morning 20 ounce bottle of Diet Mountain Dew and saw his screen still open. He had left his workstation unlocked and unattended for the first time in years. The news story with Elena Robles's picture was still on the screen. He leaned over and skimmed the article without sitting down, trying to figure out the timeline. Elena had disappeared June 3rd, almost a month ago. Donald shuddered when he realized that his nightmare of her had occurred at about that same time. What if it had been that night, the night she was killed? And what if it wasn't really a dream at all?

Donald pushed such thoughts aside as he hit Control-Alt-Delete and locked his workstation.

"You leaving?" Jeff asked, arriving back from the restroom.

"Yeah," Donald said. "I sent you over a couple of tickets. Just cell phones for a couple of new hires."

"No problem. You take it easy."

Donald left, taking the elevator down to his blue Corolla. The name Elena Robles echoed in his mind. The girl in the nightmare couldn't have been her, he told himself as he drove out of the parking garage. People didn't just dream about real people that they've never seen or met. Or perhaps Donald had seen Elena somewhere. The article said she lived in Saginaw, and Donald lived in Lewisville, in the same metro area. It was not inconceivable that their paths would have crossed. But if he had seen her somewhere why would his subconscious mind have taken such note of her?

"It really does not make sense," Donald said out loud as he turned onto the access road of State Highway 114.

What Donald had to grudgingly admit was that the nightmares had been getting worse over the past seven years, more violent, more depraved. What made the nightmares so horrendous was that it appeared to be Donald himself who was raping and killing the women in them. He saw everything through the killer's eyes, and the few times he had looked in the rear-view mirror, the face he saw was his own. Yet he was powerless to stop anything from happening. The last dream, the one with the girl who looked like Elena Robles (*it couldn't really be her*) had been the worst. He had done things to her that he couldn't even acknowledge while he was awake. It was more than unsettling that his subconscious mind could even conceive of such things. The only comforting thing about those dreams were their infrequency, coming only once every two to ten months.

Donald gave a quick thought to calling Jean to tell her that he had left work, in case she began to wonder why their daily email exchanges weren't happening as normal. But he didn't call her and didn't realize the reason for that until he passed the exit for Highway 121 north which he would have taken if he were going home. Instead, he continued west past the northern edge of DFW Airport and then turned south. If he was sick, Jean would expect him to be home. And since he wasn't going home, he figured he shouldn't call her. Instead, Donald turned on the maps app on his phone through his car's display screen.

"Holland Lake Park in Weatherford," he said, after

activating the voice command.

He saw the route trace itself on the screen and then said, "Go," to enable the navigation. The female voice told him to remain on 121 until it merged into 183.

Unlike most of what he called his normal dreams, the ones Donald referred to as the nightmare murders were vivid in every way, and he always remembered every little detail long after he had awakened. Unlike normal dreams, the memories of those nightmare murders didn't fade over time. Donald sometimes had more trouble remembering actual events than he had recalling incidents that had occurred in these nightmares. He and Jean had been married for three years when he'd had the first one. That one had started out like a regular erotic dream. The girl had been almost the opposite of Jean, black hair and smooth, dark skin as opposed to Jean's red hair and freckled pale complexion, younger and fitter than Jean who always seemed to be fighting to lose a few pounds. As he progressed to intercourse with the girl in the dream, she had started resisting until he'd had to put his hands around her throat to hold her down.

Stop thinking about it, he told himself. Recalling the details of the nightmare would only make him sick.

Given this morning's revelation, it was the victims that he had to be concerned about. If this last one had been a real person and not some figment of his imagination, then might the others have been real too? How many had there been over the last fifteen years? Without dwelling on the details, Donald started going through their faces. He counted twenty-three. Twenty-three women murdered in his subconscious. Or had they only ever lived and died there? God, he hoped so. They were a lot easier for him to dismiss when he thought they were figments of his warped imagination.

"Bullshit," he said aloud, aware that he would look like a lunatic if anyone else had been in the car with him. Just because the last nightmare victim had the same complexion and hairstyle and wore similar glasses to a girl who had just been murdered didn't mean that it was really her. So why was he driving all the way out to Weatherford? He knew the answer though. Donald had to see the place, see if anything about it seemed even a tiny bit familiar. He had to make sure that his nightmare had really been just a nightmare.

As he drove, he fought to keep the images from that last one, with the face that looked just like that photo of Elena Robles, out of his conscious thoughts. Forty minutes later, he turned right from the Interstate exit onto Holland Lake Drive. Nothing about the drive out here had seemed at all familiar, thankfully. He'd only ever been to Weatherford one time, and that had been at least a dozen years ago. Holland Lake Park was on his left with a small office building of some kind on the right. Just past the entrance to the parking lot of that office building was a Parker County Sheriff's Department patrol car parked in front of a barricade with a sign that read "Park Closed Until Further Notice". A young officer in uniform stepped out of the car and held up his hand. Donald stopped, and the deputy walked to the drivers side window.

"I'm sorry sir, but the park is closed," he said.

"Oh, OK," Donald replied.

"Do you have business here?"

"No, not really. I just wanted to see the park. Maybe walk the trails or something."

The officer looked down at Donald, seeming to take note of his business casual attire which didn't look comfortable for walking any trail. "Could I ask your name?"

"What?"

"Your name?"

"Donald White."

The deputy wrote something in a notebook.

"Do you have business here in the park?" the officer asked again.

"Business? Um, no. I was just curious. I mean, yeah, I saw what happened on the news."

"The investigation is still ongoing."

"Oh, OK."

"Did you know the victim?"

"Know her? Um, no. I didn't. I mean… No, I didn't know her."

The deputy's gaze shifted from him to his car. Donald was flustered, letting the officer intimidate him when he should be getting a sense of the place and if he had ever been here. He looked around as the deputy seemed to peer into his back seat.

Nothing here looked anywhere close to familiar which gave him a sense of relief.

"Well, OK," he said to the deputy. "I guess I'll turn around."

"All right."

The officer stepped back toward his patrol car without turning around as Donald slipped his Corolla into reverse. It took four switches from reverse to drive to reverse again before he got the Corolla pointed in the right direction. As he put it into drive the last time, he saw in his rear-view mirror the deputy snapping a photo of the Corolla with his cell phone. Feeling like he had just put his name on a suspect list for no reason, he drove back the way he had come, wondering how he'd come up with such a boneheaded idea, coming to a murder scene during an active investigation.

2

Jean White's work day had been dominated by a series of mostly useless meetings that had kept her from making much progress on either of the big projects she was managing. She had considered staying at the office to try to get at least a little work done, but her husband had uncharacteristically not answered any of the four emails she had sent him. Since she was sending and receiving email from everyone else, she wondered if his company was having email issues. He worked in IT, so she could imagine that such a thing would make for a difficult day for him. Once Jean got in the car and out of the parking garage, she called his cell.

"Hey babe," Donald answered after the second ring.

"Hey, are you OK? Where are you?"

"I'm home. I wasn't feeling well this morning."

"Oh. And you didn't call or text me?"

"I didn't want you to worry."

Something didn't sound right in the tone of Donald's voice. He'd recently been diagnosed pre-diabetic. Donald had been prescribed Metformin pills, and they'd had to change their diet. Jean thought that was a good thing, healthier for both of them, but she knew that Donald was still adjusting to the idea that he had any kind of chronic medical condition.

"Well," she said, "how are you feeling now?"

"I don't know. Are you on your way home?"

"I am."

"OK, good. I have something I want to show you."

"What is it?"

"I'll show you when you get here."

"Can you give me a hint?"

"No. I have to show you."

"Fine," she said after a pause. This, coming from someone who just said he didn't want her to worry.

"Hurry home. But be careful."

"I will," she said.

"Love you."

"Love you too, you dork." Jean disconnected the call and sighed.

When she finally did get home, she found Donald on the computer in the study. He seemed agitated. His brown hair, normally parted on his left side, was a jumbled mess, sticking up in places almost as if he had been trying to pull chunks of it from his scalp, and instead of the customary household nudity they practiced when home alone, especially during the summer months, he was still in the slacks and polo shirt he had worn to the office.

"Hey," she said to him, kissing him on the top of his head. "What time did you leave work?"

"Early. I think I was only there for fifteen minutes."

Jean walked around the corner and into their bedroom to put her bag down and empty her pockets.

"You left that early, and you didn't tell me?" she called from the bedroom. "What have you been doing all day?"

"Come here, and I'll show you."

Jean walked past the study to the laundry room, unbuttoning her blouse, intent on at least getting her accursed bra off.

"Hold on just a minute." She dropped the blouse into the hamper and unfastened her bra straps. "Ah," she said out loud in relief. Since she was right there, she went ahead and took off the rest of her clothes, throwing everything on top of her blouse.

"So how are you feeling now?" Jean asked as she walked back into the study.

She expected him to say "Fine," but he instead said, "Not good."

She put her hand to his forehead, but his temperature felt normal. "So what's the matter?"

"I think I may be losing my marbles."

"So what else is new?" she said with a laugh, but Donald swiveled the desk chair around. Jean could see the hollowness of his eyes, the skin beneath them dark. With his unkempt hair, he looked like a candidate for the asylum.

"I'm going to show you something crazy," he said. "But it's real."

"OK."

"You know those nightmares I have?"

"Yes, how could I forget?" she replied as she pulled the chair against the wall closer to him and sat down. She took his hands in hers. "Did you have another one last night?"

"No. I haven't had one in about a month."

Jean remembered the night. It had been a Saturday, and they had been at their trailer at the resort. She never slept well there with the noise of the camper's air conditioner being louder than it needed to be, and that night she'd been lying half awake, aware of Donald's mumbled thrashing and wondering if she shouldn't rouse herself enough to wake him before he bolted up into a seated position and then rolled out of the bed and stumbled to the tiny bathroom. That particular nightmare must have been rough since she had heard him sobbing in the bathroom. She knew the general nature of the dreams, that Donald saw himself doing monstrous things, but he had always refused to talk about the details with her.

He turned and pointed to the computer screen. The web browser was open to a news story about a murdered Hispanic girl. There was a photo of her embedded in the article. She leaned forward to try to read.

"That's her." Donald almost choked up as he said it.

"That's who?"

"The girl from the last nightmare."

Jean looked at the picture again. "That can't be."

"It is. And look at the date of her disappearance. It was the same night."

"How can you be sure of that?"

"We were in the trailer, so we know it was a Saturday night. I counted the weeks back, and it's that date. I'm sure of it."

Donald touched her cheek, forcing her to look at him. "Listen. This is very important. Have you ever woke up in the middle of the night, and I wasn't there?"

"What? No."

"Never?"

"No. If you're weren't in bed, you were in the bathroom. I could always hear you, and you always come right back."

Jean looked back at the photo on the screen.

"That *can't* be her," she said.

"That's what I thought at first, but I found her Facebook page." Donald reached over to the mouse and brought up another window with more photos of the same girl. "It's her. I remember that tattoo on her wrist."

About midway down the page was a photo of the inside of her wrist with a tattoo of a skull with a snake coming out of it.

"I remember the tattoo because I cut it off of her."

"*You* didn't do anything."

"In the nightmare, I did."

Jean looked back at the screen. "It can't be her."

"It is. Look at that tattoo. It can't be that common."

"Sure it can," Jean said. "It's a Death Eater logo."

"A what?"

"A Death Eater logo. From Harry Potter."

"Well, whatever it is, I took a knife and peeled the skin off her to get it."

"Stop it," Jean demanded. "You didn't do anything to her. It was a dream. A figment of your imagination."

"I know. I've always believed that ever since they started. But when I see these pictures and read about what happened to her, it doesn't feel like it. What I saw in my dream, what I saw myself do...". He shook his head.

Jean's heart almost broke at the look of horror on his face. She caressed his face, curling her hand around and running her fingers through his hair. "Did the news say that the tattoo had been cut off of her?"

"No."

"See?"

"But the police wouldn't announce those kinds of details."

Jean sighed and shook her head. "This is just a big coincidence."

"Yeah. Well then, how do you explain this?" Donald reached for the mouse and switched to a different browser tab. On the screen was another story about a murdered girl, this one in Lubbock from March of this year. "Or this?" The next tab was of a missing girl in Albuquerque, New Mexico from January. "And this?" The following tab was of a girl missing from Flagstaff, Arizona since last October and found dead in Winslow in November. "I saw those three in dreams too."

Jean shook her head, and she felt one of her tears roll down her cheek. "I don't understand."

"I saw all of them killed. I saw myself killing them."

"But you couldn't have. You were here in Texas. Flagstaff, Arizona? I mean, really?"

"I know. It doesn't make any sense." He flipped back to the tab of the girl from Albuquerque. "They never found her. In my dream, she was dumped near some kind of rock formation outside of— What was the name of the place? It was a weird sounding word." Donald closed his eyes and concentrated. "Tucumcari!" he finally said. "There was a sign that said Tucumcari 12 miles before I turned off. Maybe I should call the police there in New Mexico and tell them anonymously."

"No," Jean said, standing up and pacing around the room. "You didn't turn off any road. And you haven't been through New Mexico since our last trip to Colorado in 2017."

Donald sighed. "You're right. I couldn't have anything to do with these other three. But this last one; it was right here in our area."

"You were in our trailer all night. I know. I was awake when you got up."

"But if I can describe the place where this girl was dumped, shouldn't I tell the police? Help them find her and give just a tiny bit of peace to her family?"

"It was just a dream," Jean insisted. "You'd be wasting their time."

"But what if it did lead them to the body?"

"Then they'd think you did it."

Jean looked back at the computer screen. "Sylvia Gonzalez," she read aloud. "Did you notice that all four of those girls kind of look alike?"

"Are you saying that all Hispanic girls look alike? I know

several people who would call that racist."

"No, it's not racist. You're saying that these are the girls from your dreams, but they all look like each other. Which means that they could all look like your imaginary girl."

Donald sighed, and Jean started to feel bad for not taking him more seriously.

"I'm sorry," she said. "There has to be some kind of logical explanation for this."

"Yeah, you would think so."

Donald turned and pulled up one of his Google search results tabs, and clicked on the first unread link.

"How many of these have you gone through?" she asked.

"I don't know. A bunch. But I only found the four I recognized."

"And you've been here all day working on this?"

"Yeah."

Jean had been married to Donald for seventeen years, and the two of them had battled through their share of ups and downs. She'd always thought of him as an overgrown kid with his dry humor and little jokes, and she never knew when to take him seriously. But looking at him now, she felt, for the first time, that he might need some kind of professional help. Hell, they both may need help. But how to bring it up with him without making it worse? He was totally convinced that he had seen these murder victims in his dreams, ignoring the fact that there was no rational explanation for that.

She reached out and put her hand over his, stopping the mouse from moving, while making sure the bare nipple of her left breast touched his arm.

"How about I cook dinner while you get out of your work clothes? And then we have a nice meal in the living room. You can even turn on the Ranger game." She nodded toward the computer screen. "Let this go for a while. OK?"

Donald looked down at Jean's breast touching his forearm. "OK."

She saw the browser window go away, but she was disappointed that he had clicked the minimize button and not the X that would close the application altogether. All the tabs he had running were still open down there. Still, Jean was happy that he got up and moved away from the computer.

Even though it was his turn to cook dinner, she made spaghetti and meat sauce with spaghetti squash substituting for pasta. Donald disappeared into the bedroom, and Jean only hoped he hadn't snuck back to the computer. She was relieved when she heard the living room television power on. It was too early for the Ranger game to be on yet, but she heard Donald flipping through channels.

Once she had the squash in the oven and the meat sauce simmering, she threw a salad together. When she finished that she walked into the living room and was relieved to see a nude Donald on the couch with the remote in his hand. At least there was some sense of normalcy now. His hair, neatly brushed, appeared to be wet. He must have showered.

"It's going to be ready early," she said, "before the Ranger game. Do you want to just eat at the table?"

"That's fine," he said, setting the remote control down.

He had settled on a local newscast. Jean couldn't remember the last time they had watched the local news on television. They were running a story about funding for a high school football stadium right now, but Jean thought that Donald would have his ears out for anything new about the girl found in Weatherford.

Jean set the table, using their standard paper plates to keep down on washing dishes, and Donald took the seat where the living room television was visible. Jean retrieved the remote control and muted the sound on the way back to the table.

"Hey," Donald said, but he remained quiet after Jean gave him one of her scornful looks.

She sat down, and they clasped hands and said a quick prayer softly to themselves.

"Do you think you should see someone?" Jean asked after they had each taken a couple of bites. Donald's gaze had never left the TV.

"About what?"

Jean grabbed the remote from the table, pointed it at the living, and turned the TV off.

"You can watch that any time online," she said when Donald looked like he was about to throw a fit.

He looked from the powered off television down to his plate of spaghetti squash, and Jean saw him seem to deflate.

"Now, what do you think?"

"I don't know," he said, shaking his head, which, of course, Jean took as a big fat no.

"Why not? You don't seem to be dealing with it well on your own. Why not get a little bit of help?"

"I just don't see what good talking about it with a stranger is going to do." He took another bite, washing it down with a drink from his glass of iced tea. "Besides, they only come once every few weeks."

"And you just missed a whole day of work because of a dream you had a month ago."

"They're more than dreams now."

"And that's why you need to see someone who specializes in this."

"Fine. I'll look into it."

Jean knew her husband well enough to realize that he would do no such thing. It would be up to her to find a therapist for him and make an appointment. And that was what she intended to do.

3

Donald went to work the following day even though it was Friday, planning to tell Vanessa that his illness had just been a twenty-four hour bug or food poisoning.

"Hey, you're here," Jeff said when he arrived. "I figured you'd take a five-day weekend."

Donald started to ask about the five-day weekend thing when he realized that Monday was the Fourth of July.

"I want to try to preserve as much PTO as I can," he said. "Plus, I'm feeling a lot better."

"Any plans for the holiday weekend?" Jeff asked.

Since becoming members at the nudist resort, Donald had found it necessary to be evasive whenever anyone from work asked anything about his recreation plans, especially during summer. "We are going to try to relax by the pool with a margarita or two," he said, which was true, although Donald would drink more beers than margaritas. He had repeatedly left Jeff with the impression that he and Jean had a pool in their backyard even though they didn't.

The morning passed more slowly than most Fridays with those in the office, the ones who hadn't burned a PTO day, too interested in getting away for the long weekend than submitting Helpdesk tickets. It was a mercy when the CFO sent out an email just before eleven o'clock stating that the office would close at two for the holiday weekend.

Donald found the distraction of the Internet too much to

resist, and he spent more time checking out the news sites than working on company business. He kept waiting to see something about Elena Robles's tattoo and how it had been removed and kept by her killer, but nothing that graphic had been included in any news story. What Donald hadn't told Jean was that almost every dream had included a tattoo removal. Only one of the girls in his nightmares hadn't had a tattoo, but he had found a way to keep part of her as well, removing a section of the skin with a birthmark on her lower back. Donald supposed that the tattoo removal was one of the items that police were withholding from the public to help identify those with actual knowledge about the crime. That was why Donald couldn't just call and ask about the tattoo. Nothing would comfort him more than hearing that the tattoo on Elena's wrist, the Elena in the real world who was actually murdered, had been left alone. But in his gut, Donald knew that wasn't the case.

His shock over seeing the Elena Robles story and her photo had waned. Despite his initial fear that he had somehow actually committed the acts he had seen himself do in his nightmares, he remained convinced that he couldn't have done any of it. Still, one of the things he searched online for was a door alarm for their bedroom, something that would awaken Jean if he tried to leave. He found one called a Wander Alert Door, but seeing that it was sold by The Alzheimer's Store made him give up on the idea. Donald wasn't ready to admit that he was anywhere close to dementia.

He wondered if law enforcement had connected the cases he'd found in Arizona with the two in Texas. Surely there had to be some some kind of evidence found on or around the bodies that would tie them together. Unless they weren't connected and the fact that he had dreamed about them was just random. Maybe he should offer his services as a psychic to the police. *Psych*, about a fake psychic who was really just an exceptional detail-oriented detective, had been one of his favorite TV shows during its run.

Vanessa walked past his desk just before two o'clock. She had all her stuff with her and was obviously heading home.

"Happy Fourth," she said. "Feel free to stay and finish anything that you need to finish." Donald was able to lay off the homicide stories long enough to make sure his work was all caught up by 2:00, and he gladly left the office. He was surprised to find that Jean had beaten him home.

"Our office closed at one o'clock," Jean said when he asked her how she was home so early.

She was dressed in shorts and a t-shirt and was already packing food and drinks for the weekend. He greeted her with a kiss, got changed, and helped load her Prius with everything she had packed up.

"You can drive," she said as he locked the front door of their house.

Even though they both had keys to each other's cars, the unspoken deal they'd always had whenever they went somewhere together was that Jean would drive her Prius and Donald would drive his Corolla.

"OK," Donald said with what he hoped was a raised eyebrow.

Jean held up her phone and said, "I want to play this game."

"What game?"

"It's called Two Dots."

"Two Dots? Sounds boring."

"It's highly addictive."

Once they were on the road, Jean said, "So I found this lady named LeeAnn McDonald online."

She paused, obviously hoping Donald would say something, but all he responded with was "Uh-huh."

"She's a marriage and family therapist, but she also specializes in dreams and sleep disorders. The reviews on her are really good, and she takes our insurance."

"Like I said, I don't see what good talking about the nightmares will do."

"Just go try it out. Please. I'll go with you if you want."

Donald sighed. "Fine."

"Good. I've got you scheduled for an appointment Tuesday evening right after work."

Donald glanced over at her and shook his head.

"See, you don't even have to take any time off," she added.

"What if I have to work late that night?"

"Oh, please. When was the last time you worked late?"

Donald glanced her way and smiled. "Fine, I will do this for you."

They arrived at their travel trailer at the Bluebonnet nudist resort a little over an hour later. The first thing Donald did was plug in the power so the air conditioning would kick on. The inside of the trailer felt like a sauna. Jean put all the perishables in the fridge and the bag of ice they had bought in Decatur into the freezer. As soon as she finished undressing, she grabbed a couple of handfuls of ice from that bag, put them in the blender with some tequila and mixer. Donald undressed and grabbed his small cooler. He filled that cooler with eight cans of beer, as many as it would hold, while Jean filled her large tumbler with her newly mixed margarita. Donald dumped more of the ice into the cooler of beer. Jean draped both of their towels over her left shoulder and they both started walking toward the pool and clubhouse area together, neither of them wearing anything except sandals. Most of the members who had trailers onsite also had golf carts to get around, but Donald and Jean hadn't gotten that far in their set up yet. "Besides," Donald had said on more than one occasion, "walking is healthier."

There were about two and a half hours of daylight left, and Donald and Jean spent them either in the pool or sitting around a table talking with friends. Water volleyball was the big game at the resort, but not enough people had arrived yet to get a game going. A few of their friends disappeared a little after seven to get something to eat with most of them returning after an hour. Donald and Jean both agreed that they weren't hungry and stayed at the pool. One of the full-time residents hosted karaoke in the clubhouse every Friday night at 8:00. By then the lack of food had accentuated the effect of the alcohol they had been drinking which made karaoke fun and easygoing. Jean sang just about every song listed under Joan Jett's name.

"My name should have been Joan instead of Jean," she told Sandy, a large breasted blonde in her mid-40s sitting at the table next to theirs. She and her husband Bob were two of their best friends at the resort. Sandy's complexion was paler even than Jean's, so the two of them spent a lot of time staying out of the sun, either in the clubhouse or the shaded portion of the pool deck. When Donald and Jean had started talking about coming out to a nudist resort, Jean's biggest concern was not being able to spend as much time in the sun as everyone else, so it was fortuitous that the first couple they talked with had been Sandy and Bob.

Donald was not as brave in sharing his singing voice as Jean was. He only did two songs, and they were both ones that he could talk through rather than sing, "A Boy Named Sue" by Johnny Cash and "The Devil Went Down to Georgia" by the Charlie Daniels Band. Bob and Sandy were tired and left early, before eleven, and Donald and Jean left soon afterward, heading back to their trailer. As they walked along the gravel road, Donald was still humming Johnnie's fiddle solo when it occurred to him that he hadn't thought about Elena Robles or his nightmares once since arriving at the resort. It was no use thinking about them now, so he thought about Jean swaying back and forth on the stage as she sang "Crimson and Clover". After some clumsy drunken sex as soon as they got into the trailer, Donald and Jean both settled down to sleep. Donald drifted right off thanks to the alcohol and the physical exertion. His sleep for the night came to a sudden end a mere four hours later.

4

Jean was more asleep than awake, but she was somehow aware of her husband's noise next to her. The bed in the travel trailer was much smaller than the king sized bed they slept in at home, and Donald's thrashing around jostled her. An elbow hit her ribcage hard enough to leave a bruise, and her eyes opened. Donald grabbed her upper arm and squeezed. Jean rolled onto her back and reached across her body to try to shake Donald awake.

"Hey," she said, "let go."

"I'll fuck you so bad, you fucking cunt" he said, his voice sounding far away and not his own.

"Donald!" Jean yelled this time, grabbed his shoulder, and didn't stop shaking until his eyes were open and he was trying to fight her off.

He let go of her upper arm and sat up, pulling away from Jean's shaking, and bumping his head on a shelf above the bed. Jean rolled over and turned on the lamp next to them.

"Shit," Donald said, rubbing the spot where the top of his head had struck.

"It was one of those dreams, wasn't it?" Jean asked, sitting up in bed beside him but with enough grace to not bump her head.

"Yeah," he managed to say between breaths.

He was trembling, and Jean took his hand in hers to try to give him some sense of normalcy and calm. Donald pulled his hand away.

"You shouldn't touch me," he said. "I'm not right in the head."

Jean had to restrain herself from putting her hands on his shoulders. "Do you want to talk about it?"

Donald shook his head and crawled over her to get out of the bed. He stood in what passed for a kitchen in the travel trailer, still panting, his hands trembling.

"At least you and the therapist will have something new to talk about," she said, trying to use humor to lighten things. She knew that was the wrong move before she even finished saying it. Donald walked over to the door and slipped his sandals on.

"Where are you going?"

"A walk," he grunted and walked out of the trailer. He didn't even take a towel with him.

Jean sighed and rolled out of bed. She slipped on her sarong and sandals, grabbed a flashlight and a towel for Donald, and stepped outside. The breeze was cooler than she would have expected for a July night in Texas. She could see Donald's silhouette on the gravel road between the trailer and the pool deck as he continued to walk away from her. Jean decided not to turn the flashlight on if she could help it. She would be walking past six trailers, at least two of them with people sleeping inside, and she didn't want anyone disturbed by a bobbing light out their windows. She also didn't want Donald to realize that she was following him. He walked through the gate of the pool enclosure and onto the deck, heading toward the hot tub. Jean tripped and almost fell as she tried to step onto the brick path to the pool. She caught her balance and heard the jets of the hot tub start up as she opened the gate.

The hot tub was in a screened-in covered patio next to the building that housed the showers and restrooms and the pumps for the two pools. Jean stood at the screen door and watched her husband sitting in the jacuzzi, his arms extended on the edge of the tub, his head back and his face pointed almost straight up to the ceiling. She had a sudden image of him falling asleep and slipping under the water and drowning. Donald opened one eye when she opened the screen door and walked in, letting it slam back shut.

"You just felt like soaking in a hot tub?" Jean said as she simultaneously slipped the sarong off, letting it fall onto a plastic chair, and pulled her feet from her sandals. She dropped the towel she'd brought for Donald on top of her sarong and walked down the steps to sit in the water next to him.

"I had to sit down somewhere, and I forgot to bring a towel."

"Wow, this water's hot."

"Yeah, I had to take the cover off before I got in," Donald said. "I guess it just simmers all night under it."

Jean inched her way into the near scalding water next to him, and Donald pulled himself up straighter and let his arms fall into the water.

"Sorry," he said. "For grabbing you. I've never done that before, have I?"

"No." She paused and then needlessly asked, "Was it bad?"

Donald nodded. "It was getting even worse. Thank you for waking me up."

She thought about how tightly he had squeezed her arm. What if that had been her neck? She thought about what he had said, using words that she had never heard him say before while he was awake, fuck and cunt, and for the first time wondered if she had any cause for concern about her own safety during these episodes? She was never more glad that she had made that therapist appointment for him.

"Was it the same as last month?" Jean asked.

"No. They're all a little different. New girl. New place."

He stopped, staring at the timer switch for the hot tub bubbles as it clicked back down. The max setting was fifteen minutes. Donald must not have turned it all the way as there looked to be only a minute or two left. Jean took comfort in the fact that there were always several weeks between these nightmare episodes. Now that he'd had this one, they should be good for at least another month. At least, she hoped so.

"Are you going to come back to bed?" Jean asked.

They both looked at the clock on the wall. It was almost five AM now.

"I doubt it."

"You'll be boiled like a lobster if you stay in here the rest of the night."

"I won't be able to go back to sleep," he said. "I mean, could you?"

"I doubt it. At least come back to the trailer with me. Lay down. I'll take the side against the wall and you can have the outside.

Jean felt a sense of relief when Donald said, "OK." They waited where they sat, listening to the jacuzzi bubbles until the timer dinged.

"I wish I'd brought two towels," Jean said when the cool air hit her wet skin as she stepped out.

"Here," Donald said, handing her the towel. "I'll be dry before we get to the trailer," he added when she hesitated.

The screen door opened, and an older man walked in with a towel slung over his shoulder.

"Oh, hello," he said.

He was one of the people Jean saw at the resort all the time, but she couldn't remember his name.

"Hey Bob," Donald said.

"I'm usually the only one in the hot tub this early," he said.

"We were just heading out," Donald said.

"Don't run off on my account."

"We're going to try to get some more sleep. But we'll see you around all weekend?"

"I'll be here," Bob said and sighed as he stepped into the hot water. "That's hot."

Jean finished toweling herself dry and offered it back to Donald. He shook his head. After wrapping the sarong and the towel over her neck, they walked hand in hand along the gravel road.

"Now which Bob was that?" Jean asked. The resort had so many members named Bob that they had to give nicknames to each one. Sandy's Bob was known as Bald Bob, and Jean could think of a Sponge Bob, a Beaver Bob, and a Brown Bob.

"That was Handyman Bob, I think," Donald said.

He seemed to be dry well before they walked into the trailer and got back into bed. Jean didn't know how long she lay there watching Donald play some game on his cell phone before she drifted back to sleep. He was still next to her and still on his phone when she woke up with the sun shining through the trailer's windows. She propped herself up on an elbow to get a glimpse of his screen and saw the partially loaded page of one of the Dallas-Fort Worth news stations.

"Come on," she heard him whisper in frustration as he waited on the page to load.

"Did you get any more sleep?" she asked.

"No."

She lay back down, thanking God that it was a long holiday weekend and that they were here at the camp among friends.

"Are you going to be able to relax and have fun today?"

"I'll try," he replied.

I sure hope that therapist has some magic that will coax him into talking, she thought.

As it turned out, Donald did seem to be his regular self when sitting at the pool, playing water volleyball, or just riding around with Bald Bob on his and Sandy's golf cart. Bald Bob even let Donald drive a few times. They planned on getting their own golf cart eventually even though they did both enjoy walking, so they figured they ought to get used to riding around on one. The only time that weekend Jean really wished they already had a cart was when they had to walk from the trailer to the clubhouse carrying the crock pot full of her ham, green beans, and potato dish on Saturday evening for the weekly potluck. After dinner, they stayed in the clubhouse for the weekly dance. Some of the women liked to dress in some kind of lingerie or other minimal outfit. Jean always liked to just stay nude. If one were going to stay at a nudist resort and dance, why not enjoy it with that same sense of freedom that brought them to the resort in the first place? One could go to a conventional nightclub and dance in skimpy outfits any weekend.

When they finally got back to the trailer, they were not as drunk as the previous night. But Donald's lack of sleep the previous night seemed to have caught up with him, and he crashed hard, snoring heavily. It was Jean who stayed awake and on her phone this time. The signal for data was not good, and the resort's wifi was centered in the clubhouse and didn't reach down to their trailer. So rather than frustrate herself by trying to get a webpage to load like Donald had done that morning, she played games while she ruminated on Donald's nightmares.

She knew, of course, that the girl whose body they found in Weatherford couldn't have been in his dream any more than those other three girls could. The problem was that Donald believed he had seen them. Jean supposed that he thought he was seeing some kind of psychic visions through his dreams now, despite the fact that he could not point to anything and prove that he had seen it beforehand. If she could have gotten him to tell her some specifics about the dream last night, she could have headed off whatever news story he later found and said had been a part of that dream. Even as she thought this, she hated that she was doubting her husband like this. But the things he had been talking about the last two days were impossible. There had to be some other explanation. The fact was that the only person who knew what Donald saw in his dreams was Donald. She wished she could give him some benefit of the doubt, but these things were too outlandish to be real.

Last night had frightened her. Never before had Donald grabbed her in his sleep like that. If he thought he was violent in his dreams, should she be concerned that he might become violent in real life? She could never believe that. He was always the kindest, gentlest man she had ever met, always eager to hold a baby at family get togethers, both his family and hers. He even refused to go hunting because he didn't have the heart to kill an animal. No, his grabbing of her arm was him trying to stop something, hold something back. That HAD to be it.

5

The holiday weekend afforded Donald and Jean the novelty of spending three nights in a row in the travel trailer. Sunday was another day of lounging, drinking, water volleyball, and just floating in the pool with friends. But as relaxing as Sunday was, Friday's nightmare still haunted Donald. The girl had been latina like the ones in the other dreams, but this one had hair that had been dyed a bright fire engine red. She had already been tied up and gagged in the back seat of a car when the dream started. Donald was driving, and he remembered passing a Seven-Eleven and Wendy's, then a Chase Bank and a Wal-mart, followed by something else, something enormous and white and silver, dwarfing all the structures around it. A vast empty parking lot surrounded it. It wasn't until he was in the hot tub after Jean had woken him up that he had realized that it had been AT&T Stadium in Arlington.

The girl kept whimpering and crying in the back seat, and every time Donald saw his face in the rear view mirror— it was his face and not someone else's—he had been grinning. The dream had lasted longer than usual, with a lot of driving. He had turned onto an old dirt road, driven for a few more miles before stopping, and dragged the girl out of the back seat and into a grassy area. She had kicked at him until he grabbed an ankle and drove a knife through her foot. He did other things after that, things that he did not want to even consider while awake. Donald was just glad that Jean had pulled him out of the dream before it got worse. He had been afraid to go to sleep the following night, but the exhaustion had caught up with him. He fell asleep well before he meant to, but he was happy that the dream didn't recur. That was the only good thing about those nightmares; they only came once.

He and Jean left the resort late Monday morning and arrived home a little after noon. Jean took a nap which left Donald to himself. Rather than sit around the house waiting for Jean to wake up so that they could figure out where they were going to watch fireworks, he got in his car and drove toward Arlington. He had seen nothing on the news about a girl missing or killed from Arlington, but he knew that it was only a matter of time. He drove down Collins, seeing a couple of Seven-Eleven's and the back of the Walmart that was just before AT&T Stadium. Nothing flared in his memory, so he turned around at Division Street and drove up Collins the other direction. Still nothing, so he turned west at Interstate 30 and drove all the way out to Fort Worth. His phone rang just as he passed downtown. When he saw that it was Jean, he almost didn't answer it. But he decided against ignoring her and hit the phone button on his car's screen.

"Hey."

"Hey, where are you?" she asked.

"Just driving around," he said, unable to think of anything on the fly that would sound better.

"Are you OK?"

"Yeah, I'm fine. I'll be home in a little bit. I just felt like going to the bookstore."

"Ok, be careful. I love you."

"Love you too."

He disconnected the call before she did and kept driving. When he passed the Camp Bowie exit, he knew he was getting close to the Ridgmar Mall area and the spot where Elena Robles's abandoned car had been found. He was thirsty, so he took the Ridglea exit and stopped at a gas station just off the freeway. There wasn't much of a parking lot for cars who didn't need gas, and he didn't want to take up one of the pumps. Donald took what may or may not have been an actual parking spot at the side of the building and wandered inside.

"Hey," the clerk said when he walked in.

"Hi," Donald replied before turning for the soft drink cooler.

He pulled a Diet Mountain Dew from the rack and took it to the counter.

"Diet Mountain Dew?" the clerk said. "That's not your usual."

"I'm sorry, what?"

"Your usual. Real sugar Dr. Pepper."

"What are you talking about?"

"I don't know," the clerk said, with a perplexed look on his face. "My mistake."

"I can't drink real sugar Dr. Pepper. I was diagnosed as pre-diabetic two months ago."

"Two months ago? You bought a Dr. Pepper Saturday night."

"You saw me Saturday night?"

"Yeah, sure."

"Like, the night before last? That Saturday night?"

"Yeah. I mean, I think so."

Donald felt a strange tickling in his gut, and his heart seemed to beat faster. He was certain he had never been in this store before. Or had he?

"How often do you see me here?" Donald asked.

"What?"

"How often do you see me in here?"

The clerk looked up at the ceiling. "About three or four nights a week, I guess."

"Nights?"

"Yeah. I usually work the second shift, but I came in early today, for the holiday."

"So it was before eleven?" Donald said.

"Yeah, I guess so."

"How long have I been coming in here three or four nights a week?"

"What, you don't know?"

"Humor me."

The clerk shrugged. "I don't know. I've only worked here six months, but all of those."

"Three times a week? And always at night, before eleven o'clock?"

"Yeah, I guess so."

"Do I drive, or do I walk?"

"Fuck, I don't know dude. You tell me."

Donald put exact change down on the counter, took his Diet Mountain Dew, and walked back to his car, wondering what that was all about. The clerk had to have been mistaken. Even if Donald had been here once without remembering, there was no way he could have come in three times a week, much less three times total. Shaking his head, he got in the car, took a big drink from his Diet Mountain Dew, and drove back onto the freeway. He looked at the right shoulder of the road as he passed the Ridgmar Mall, but nothing seemed familiar at all. Once he got past the mall, he punched the home button on his maps app and followed the directions back to the house.

Jean was sitting on the sofa waiting for him. She was dressed, which meant that she expected to be going somewhere soon. Her expression was stern like that of the miniature statue of Athena on the end table next to her. Her grandmother had carved the statue in marble decades ago.

"Everything all right?" she asked.

"Yeah," he said. "I didn't feel like napping, and I didn't want to disturb you."

"Did you see anything good at the bookstore?"

"Oh yeah. Lots and lots of stuff. But you'll be happy to know that I didn't buy anything."

"Well, that's good, I guess."

"Sure it is."

She sighed and stood up. Donald sensed trouble, so he tried to think of something to say to diffuse it.

"Do you want to go to Fort Worth to see the Concert in the Gardens fireworks show?" Jean asked before he could get anything out.

"I don't know. It's kind of far, and we have to work tomorrow."

"OK. Are there any fireworks shows closer?"

"Sure. There's Victory Plaza, but getting in and out of there is such a pain."

"We could just go to dinner then."

Donald shrugged. "OK. Is that why you're dressed? You just have to get out of the house?"

"I got dressed two hours ago, Donald. I thought we would spend the day off together, but instead you disappeared."

"I'm sorry." Donald decided that he really didn't have anything that he needed to be dishonest about, and maybe opening up to her would diffuse her apparent anger at him. "There was something I wanted to look at. A couple of things, actually."

"And what were those?" When Donald hesitated, she said, "Dream stuff?"

"Yeah."

Jean sighed. "Baby, you have to quit obsessing about that." She walked across the room and sat down on the love seat.

Donald followed her and sat next to her. "I can't help it."

"I know you. You obsess about things all the time, but you have to make yourself step back and take a deep breath and not let this thing consume you."

"I don't obsess about things."

"Do you remember the two weeks where we listened to nothing but the *Les Miserables* soundtrack? Or the money you poured into that DVD collection. How many people have copies of every Oscar Best Picture in chronological order on their shelf?"

"It is a cool collection," Donald said when he couldn't think of any other comeback. "I don't know of anyone else who has one."

"That's beside the point. What I don't want to see happen is you obsess over these dreams to the point that you have them more often. You already have so much trouble those nights when you do have one."

"So why should I go see a therapist about them?" Donald asked. "If you want me to stop thinking about them?"

"I didn't say don't think about them. I said stop obsessing about them. You don't need to go searching for clues in the real world about something that happens in that head of yours." When Donald started to say something, Jean continued. "I know you have convinced yourself that those girls, those victims in the news, were from your dreams. But they are dreams. They are vague even while you're in them. And they fade over time. At least they should."

"I've told you many times, these dreams are different. They

feel real while I'm in them, and after I wake up. I remember every detail. I know. I have regular dreams too on occasion, and these are nothing like that. It scares me to think that they may not just be dreams. They're more like visions." He thought about telling her about the convenience store clerk who thought he knew Donald, but he decided not to. He still didn't know what to think of that himself.

"That's why you need to see someone who specialized in this kind of thing. You *are* going tomorrow, right?"

Donald nodded. Jean had already made the appointment, and it couldn't hurt to talk with someone with experience.

"Good," she said. "Now lets get in the car and go see some fireworks."

"Where?"

"I don't care. You pick."

6

The fifth of July was a Tuesday, but it felt more like a Monday. Once the working day ended, Donald drove straight to a small one story office building just a few miles away. A middle-aged woman was sitting in the waiting area of the building lobby reading a book. They gave each other a cursory smile in acknowledgement before she returned to her book. Donald walked past her and found the door for the office of LeeAnn McDonald on which was a sign saying, "In Session, do not disturb. Please wait in building lobby." Donald turned around and sat in a chair across from the woman, wishing he had brought a book of his own to read. The building directory on the wall near the door listed the tenants and their suite numbers. Besides McDonald counseling, there was an attorney, a massage therapist, and a public relations firm. A massage sounded nice right about then. Donald had never had a professional massage. He walked down the hall to the massage therapist's suite, but her door was closed. He stood close and listened, wondering if she might also be in a session or just not in the office. There was no music coming from inside that he could hear, so he assumed she was gone. Donald sat back down in the building lobby and surfed the web on his phone until a teenage boy walked out of the door of McDonald Counseling.

"Mom?" the boy said, and the lady with the book got up and disappeared into LeeAnn McDonald's office.

Donald remained in the waiting area and couldn't help wondering what issues the kid was having. Could it be dreams? But this LeeAnn McDonald specialized in more than just dream therapy. Maybe the kid was having problems coping in school. Or maybe he was into drugs. Donald shook his head and told himself to stop thinking about the kid. Whatever issues he had were none of his business.

The teenager and the mom came out of the office a moment later, the mom thanking LeeAnn for everything she was doing, and walked out into the hot July sunshine. LeeAnn had an athletic build with shoulder length dirty blonde hair. Her arms, visible because of the yellow sleeveless blouse, were heavily freckled, and he thought those freckles might also cover her face if not for the coat of makeup she wore.

"Mr. White?" she said when she saw him sitting outside her office.

"Yes." He stood.

"I'm LeeAnn." She spoke with a southern drawl, not uncommon in Texas. "Do you go by Don or Donnie?"

"The only people who call me Don are at the office. Family all call me Donald."

"OK, Donald. Come on in. Feel free to call me LeeAnn."

Donald walked into a cozy office with two framed certificates on the wall, a desk in the corner, a small swivel chair on wheels like a medical doctor might have in an examining room, and a Lazy-Boy recliner. On the wall opposite the two certificates was a framed photograph of a scenic mountain landscape.

"Please have a seat," LeeAnn said, motioning to the recliner.

They both sat, and LeeAnn clicked through a few screens on the laptop on her desk. "Good, you've filled everything out online."

"That would have been my wife."

She turned and looked at him. "Does that mean you weren't exactly on board with coming here?"

Donald shrugged. "I don't know. I just—I don't know how you can help me with my problem."

"Well, why don't you explain what that is, and we'll see what kind of help I can offer."

"It's kind of unusual."

LeeAnn nodded. "Don't worry about that. There are no judgments here. Just tell me what the issues are, and then we'll try to deal with them."

Donald took a deep breath and started. "Every few weeks, I have a nightmare. Different nightmares. They are very vivid and very violent. In them, I see myself take a young girl and do things to her. Things that—" He stopped, not knowing how to verbalize what he saw himself do in these dreams. Donald had never told Jean the details. Since Jean was his only confidante, that meant that he had never told anyone, which also meant that he had never verbalized any of those details. He wasn't sure he could.

"What things?" LeeAnn said. She had her laptop in her lap and was typing just a few notes but kept most of her attention on Donald.

He didn't see any way out of just stating it matter of factly, so he said, "I rape them and kill them."

"In the same way?"

"It generally follows a pattern, yes."

"How?"

"I don't think I should go into that."

"I think you should," LeeAnn said. "You can't confront your issue if you don't acknowledge it."

"You don't understand."

"I don't understand what?"

"How.." He trailed off searching for the right word. "Evil. How evil they are."

LeeAnn sat in silence for a moment, her eyes on Donald. "Try telling me what happens in third person if that helps," she finally said. "Take yourself out of it. I need to know what you're experiencing if I'm going to help you."

Donald took a deep breath. "OK. They are all a little different, of course, but it usually starts with the girl already tied up. Sometimes she's in the back of the car. Other times, she's already at the place."

"The place?"

"Yeah. The place where she's raped and killed."

"What is this place like?"

"They're all different. Different places."

LeeAnn typed a few more things onto her laptop. "Are

there any shared characteristics between these places."

Donald nodded. "Yeah. They're all outside. In the woods. Or shrubs around if it's in a desert."

"So the locales change?"

"Yeah."

She looked up at him. "Anything else?"

"No. Like I said, they're all different."

LeeAnn took a deep breath. Donald thought it might have been a sigh. He looked at the door of her office, wondering if she'd charge him if he just got up and walked out.

"So what happens at these places?"

"The girl is raped and killed."

"By you?"

"I thought I was supposed to tell you in third person."

A smirk appeared on LeeAnn's face. "You're right. Sorry. How is that done, exactly?"

"I don't think you want to hear the details."

"I probably don't, but I need to if I'm to help you. And you probably need to tell me. I suppose you haven't told your wife these details."

"No."

LeeAnn typed more on her laptop. "Go ahead."

"He takes a knife and cuts the clothes off her. The girl usually tries to scream, but there's always some kind of gag in her mouth, sometimes just a rag tied down with a rope around her head, but with the last couple, I've— there's been an actual ball gag, like in a BDSM store. Once she's naked, he runs the knife around, the tip nipping her in a few places, bad enough to draw little droplets of blood."

Donald stopped, waiting for LeeAnn to make more notes, but she just sat and looked at him.

"And then?"

"It gets sexual."

"How so?"

Donald cleared his throat. "You don't want to hear that."

"But I need to hear it."

"Okay. I enter her. I mean, he enters her. Intercourse, you know."

LeeAnn nodded.

"Most of them struggle against it, but some of them just lie there with their eyes closed, hoping it will be over soon, I guess. When he comes— You know. Just before, I guess, he sticks the knife in between two ribs and into her heart. It's like, the blood needs to spurt out of her when I — you know."

LeeAnn typed a few notes in her laptop and was silent for a few moments. "And you said this isn't the same recurring dream?"

"No. The girls are different. The places are different. Sometimes different things happen. I hear things that make me stop sometimes."

"And when you climax in the dream, do you actually climax?"

Donald's first impulse is to say no, of course not. Because that would be weird and awful. But the fact is that he did find evidence on his sheets the next morning.

"It's all right if you do," LeeAnn prompted.

"Not every time," he finally said, more to save face than anything else.

"I don't suppose you're wearing a condom in these dreams?"

"No."

She typed a few more notes and said, "Tell me about these girls. You said they were different every time. But is there some trait they have in common?"

"They all seem to be Hispanic. Young, black hair, dark skin, brown eyes."

"Young Latino women. Every time?"

"Yes," Donald said, nodding.

"You said you have one of these dreams every few weeks?"

"Yes."

"How many weeks?"

"Sometimes two; sometimes nine or ten."

"Irregular intervals then." She typed another note. "You said the victims are all Hispanic. Do they share any other characteristics."

Donald took a moment to think and slowly shook his head. "No."

"Hmmm." LeeAnn typed another note on her laptop. "Why do you think they're all Latina?"

Donald shrugged. "Your guess is as good as mine."

"Is your wife Latina?" she asked as she continued to type.

Donald shook his head. "No, she's of a very white Irish descent."

"No ex-girlfriends?"

"Nope, none that I can recall."

LeeAnn seemed to finish typing and looked up at Donald. "When you have one of these dreams, what happens?"

"I already told you what happens."

"I don't mean in the dream; I mean in the real world. Do you wake up screaming or in a sweat, or do you go on sleeping?"

"Oh, I wake up. Jean, my wife, she usually gets woken up too. So yeah, I guess I wake up screaming or making some kind of sound."

"Do you go back to sleep afterwards?"

"Oh no. I'm done sleeping after I have one of those. But like I said, they only happen once every few weeks. So it's not like I never get any sleep."

"When was the last time you had one of these dreams?"

Donald sighed. "Just a couple of nights ago, but Jean woke me up before it got really bad. Thank God. We weren't at home, so maybe she wasn't sleeping well."

"Where were you?"

"In our trailer out at Bluebonnet."

"What's Bluebonnet?"

Donald gave a short little laugh. He wasn't used to telling people about his and Jean's summer weekends. "It's a nudist resort out near Decatur."

"Oh really! Wow, that's interesting. You have a trailer there, you said?"

"Yes."

LeeAnn sat studying Donald until he began to wonder if she wasn't trying to picture him without his clothes. "How long have you been going there?" she finally asked.

"This is our first year as full members. We went out a couple of times last year."

"Whose idea was it to visit the first time? Yours or your wife's?"

"Mine, but Jean wound up enjoying it as much as I did, if not more."

"How did you bring it up? It seems rather unusual, going to a nudist resort."

"It only seems unusual to people who've never considered it."

"Do you think going to such a place contributes to the erotic nature of your dreams?"

Donald shook his head. "It's the other way around. I had thought that some of the porn I used to watch on the Internet might have had something to do with the dreams, and that made me want to quit watching it. But quitting that porn was not easy when it's just right there all the time."

"In my experience, overcoming pornography addiction is one of the most difficult things a person can try to do."

Donald thought of the kid who had been here before him and wondered if that was one of his problems. "I wanted to try a nudist resort because I thought that if I could somehow demystify the body, desexualize it if you will, that the allure of pornography would go away. So I sought out a venue where that could be done."

"Interesting. What gave you that idea?"

"A Christian website called MyChainsAreGone.org."

"A Christian website?" LeeAnn asked as she typed something else onto her laptop. "And did it work? Were you able to stay away from the porn sites?"

"Yeah, it did work, surprisingly enough. I never even have the urge to look at any porn sites anymore. But, of course, the dreams continued."

"Was the pornography you used to watch violent?"

Donald shook his head. "No, it was pretty much typical sex."

LeeAnn typed a few more notes before looking back up at Donald.

"A lot of people have dreams about a monster or a boogie man, but it's very unusual for someone to see themselves as that monster."

Donald shrugged.

"Have you talked to any family about these dreams? Is anyone else having them?"

Donald shook his head. "The only person I've told about the dreams is Jean. And now you, of course."

LeeAnn typed another quick note.

"You don't think it would be faster to use a pen and paper?" Donald said.

"No, not for me. Did you suffer any trauma as a child?"

Donald shook his head.

"No abusive parents or other family members? Babysitters?"

"No, nothing I can remember."

LeeAnn made another note. "Were you an only child?"

"Yes. And I was adopted. My parents could never have biological children."

"Are your parents still together?"

"No. Dad died in a car accident five years ago."

"Oh. I'm sorry to hear that."

Donald shrugged again. "It was an awful shock, but, what are you gonna do?"

The staccato of LeeAnn's typing sped up, and Donald could see that she was right. Typing for her was faster than writing.

"Have you ever tried to find your birth parents?"

Donald sighed. "Not really. I was just diagnosed as pre-diabetic, and my wife thought it would be helpful to send my DNA off to Ancestry.com or whatever it is to try to get a family medical history."

"And what did that reveal?"

Donald shrugged. "We're still waiting for the results."

"Are you hoping that the test will lead you to your birth family?"

Donald shrugged again. "I don't know. I guess it will if someone there also sent their DNA to Ancestry."

LeeAnn nodded and made more notes.

"Did you tell your mother you submitted your DNA?"

Donald shook his head. "No."

"Why not?"

"I don't know. I asked her about my birth mom once, when I was a teenager. She couldn't tell me much. Said it was a closed adoption. And she seemed hurt or sad that I had asked."

"It's only natural that someone in your shoes would want to learn something about his birth parents. She should realize that."

"Yeah, I guess. But she was…. I don't know. She seemed very sensitive about the subject."

"If your DNA sample comes back and leads you to your birth parents, are you going to tell her about it?"

"I don't know. Probably not."

"Well, I would encourage you to talk with your mother about everything. Like I said, it's only natural you would want to know about your heritage, especially if you have any medical concerns. She should be understanding."

"You don't know my mother."

LeeAnn gave him a smile. Her questions then focused more on the dreams themselves and what had prompted him to finally seek professional help. Donald told her about recognizing the photo of a recent murder victim as the girl in one of his nightmares and then finding the photos of two more victims in other states.

"You don't suspect you somehow committed these crimes in your sleep, do you?" LeeAnn asked in a slightly higher pitched voice. It was the first time he had detected even a tiny bit of emotion in anything she said or did.

"No, I couldn't have," Donald answered. "I'm always in bed when I wake up, and Jean is always there."

"OK, good," LeeAnn said with a forced smile, "because that would have been a different issue altogether."

Donald shrugged at that, wishing he'd never brought it up. After a few more questions that Donald found mostly pointless, as if LeeAnn were on a fishing expedition, she announced that their time was up.

"Already," Donald said. He was thankful that LeeAnn didn't seem to detect the sarcasm in his voice.

"Would you like to keep this same appointment next week?"

"Um," Donald hesitated, "I'll have to talk to my wife and check my calendar."

LeeAnn looked at him in silence for a few seconds before turning and grabbing a business card from the desk behind her. "My schedule fills up quickly so I recommend you call by tomorrow."

Donald took the card and slipped it into his front pants pocket. "Will do."

7

For a brief moment, Jean was surprised that she had beaten Donald home before remembering that he had gone to the appointment that she had set for him. She hoped it was going well, and she prayed that Donald did not just clam up like he usually did. When Jean got in the house, she pulled what she needed for dinner out of the fridge, setting it all on the kitchen counter, and went to the computer in their bedroom. After getting out of her work clothes, she checked their joint email and saw that a notification of a new message on the Ancestry account was waiting for her.

Jean went straight to Ancestry and logged in as Donald since that's the account she had used to submit his DNA sample. "Your results are in," the message in the inbox read. She clicked the link in the message and got a list of ethnicities and of names. Only one name was within two degrees of relation, either a grandparent or an aunt or uncle. That name, Barbara Janney, was a hyperlink, so Jean clicked on it. Barbara Janney's information page came up along with her public family tree. The names of the relatives still living were not present, but it did show that she had two daughters and one son. One of the daughter's names was visible, Nancy Ann Janney, with the dates 1962 - 2007 beneath that name. Each of her children had one or two children listed, but no other names were visible. The names of Barbara's parents were there, along with her grandparents and most of her great grandparents. Barbara had no siblings, at least according to what was on her family tree.

There was a link to send Barbara Janney a direct message, and Jean clicked it. She typed "Dear Barbara" and then deleted "Barbara" and typed "Ms. Janney". How should she start such a message out of the blue? She intended to write it out but to wait for Donald to read it before hitting send. It took her a moment to get her thoughts together, and then she started typing.

We are Donald and Jean White from Lewisville, TX. Your name came up as a possible close relative in the results of Donald's DNA test. He was adopted as an infant, and his birth family has remained unknown to us. Donald was recently diagnosed as pre-diabetic which got us wondering about his family medical history in general. So we submitted the DNA test on Ancestry in the hopes of learning some of that history. He was born on April 2, 1979 in Shreveport, Louisiana. If that date tells you anything about who might be his birth parents, please let us know. Thank you.

Jean looked at what she had typed. It seemed too short for an introductory letter, but it spelled out the basic information. If this Barbara Janney had a close family member who had ever given up a baby for adoption around that date and location and had ever been curious about whatever had happened to that baby, she ought to answer. Still, she thought about adding something more about Donald and the life he'd led. But if Barbara Janney knew nothing about Donald's adoption or for some reason didn't want any contact with him, then such information would be useless. And Jean hoped that the lack of information might spark her curiosity and make a reply more likely.

Jean sighed, got up, and went to the kitchen to start dinner. Donald arrived home while she was slicing the zucchini. She had already sliced the yellow squash and chopped one green and one red bell pepper and thrown them into the casserole dish along with the olive oil and Cajun seasoning. Once she finished the zucchini, she'd slice two pounds of Andouille sausage and throw in a bag of jumbo shrimp. The oven was already preheating, and when she had everything mixed in the dish, she'd put it in and wait. It was a simple but tasty recipe, one she had found on a Keto website while looking for healthier options after Donald's blood sugar problem became evident.

Donald's first stop was the kitchen, standing behind her and caressing her bare hip.

"Looks good," he said as he kissed her neck.

"Are you talking about the dinner?"

"Maybe."

"Mmm-hmm. How was the appointment?"

Donald stopped kissing her neck but left his hand on her hip. "It was."

"Did you set a second appointment?"

"No."

"Why not?" She lifted the cutting board and slid the sliced zucchini into the casserole dish.

Donald shrugged. "I don't think she can help me."

"You think that after one appointment? You're not giving it a chance. Did you even talk to her?"

"I did."

Jean ripped open the bag of shrimp and dumped it into the pan. "Did you really talk to her?"

Donald moved around to her side with his back to the kitchen counter. "I said I did. I told her all about the dreams. All the bloody details."

A long andouille sausage flopped out onto the counter as Jean peeled open its package. "And what did she say?"

"Nothing much. A bunch of therapist babble. But she did seem concerned when I told her I found the victims on the news."

Jean started slicing the sausage, and Donald grabbed the end piece and tossed it into his mouth.

"Well, who wouldn't be," she said. "Oh, we got your Ancestry results back."

"And?" Donald asked.

"We got a hit on someone who may be a close relative. I wrote her a message. It's on the computer. If it looks OK to you, go ahead and hit send."

"All right." Donald gave her cheek a quick kiss and went to check the message.

"Yeah, that sounds good," Donald called from the bedroom a minute later.

"Then hit send," Jean called back as she dumped the first pound of sausage into the casserole dish.

"So I'm only fourteen percent Irish," Donald called.

"Yeah, I thought it would be more than that."

"You are definitely more than fourteen percent."

"Do you think I should send them my DNA?"

"Why not," Donald replied.

She shrugged as she started slicing the second pound of sausage even though Donald wasn't in the room to see her. "Maybe I will."

Jean heard Donald's phone ring.

"Hey Mom," he said as he walked back into the kitchen, having undressed.

"Donny," his mother said through the speaker phone, "how are you feeling?" She was the only person Donald allowed to call him Donny.

"I feel fine." Donald laid the phone at the kitchen table and sat in one of the chairs. "You're on speaker, by the way."

"Hi Nancy," Jean said.

"Hello Jean."

"Why are you asking how I'm feeling?"

"Because I've caught the worst summer cold I can remember," she said with a sniffle.

"Oh, I'm sorry." Donald looked up at Jean and shrugged. "Does that mean you're not coming to dinner tomorrow?"

"I think I should skip it, yes. I just don't feel well enough to drive all that way."

Jean dumped the second pound of sliced andouille into the pan and used her hands to mix everything together, relieved that her mother-in-law wasn't coming tomorrow and feeling a bit guilty that she felt such relief. The Cajun seasoning was sticking to the wet sides of the squash, and she was trying to get it to spread evenly throughout the dish.

"Well, we'll miss you," Donald said. "I did —"

"I used to never get sick every month, but ever since Covid, it's been like this. I'm sorry, what were you about to say?"

Jean stifled a laugh. For two years, Nancy had been blaming any ailment anyone had on Covid.

"What was I about to say?" Donald said. "Oh yeah, I wanted to tell you about you this thing I did on the computer."

Jean pulled her hands from the casserole dish and moved to the sink to wash them. She gave Donald a questioning look, as if to say *Are you sure you want to tell your mother this?* But she remained silent.

Donald looked back at her and nodded as he began speaking. "I told you about my blood sugar issue."

"Yes, you need to keep a careful watch on that."

"I am, Mom. I've also been having some issues sleeping, and I was wondering if there was anything else I might need to worry about. Because I was adopted, I don't know anything about any family medical history. So we sent my DNA off to Ancestry.com for analysis."

"Hold on." Nancy coughed a couple of times, and Jean could hear her blow her nose. "Sorry. Will that give you your medical history?"

"No, but it does list my ethnicity. Did you know that I'm fourteen percent Irish?"

"I thought it would be more than that."

"We did too. No, it gives you that, but it also lists potential family members, but only if they've also submitted DNA to Ancestry."

"And has anyone submitted their DNA?"

'Actually yes. I got one name back. Not a parent but a possible aunt or grandparent. We've written her a message."

"Did she write back?"

"Not yet."

The line was silent for a moment. Donald looked up at Jean with a raised eyebrow.

"Well," Nancy finally said, "you let me know if she writes back. I'd like to know about your family medical history too. You are my son after all, and I worry about you."

Jean heard a bit of an emphasis on the words "my son". She looked at Donald who raised his eyebrow again.

"I know you do," he said to the phone.

"And be careful. Don't let anyone scam you."

Jean shook her head at Donald who suppressed a laugh.

"I won't. Now you rest and get to feeling better."

"I will. I love you Donny."

"I love you too."

Donald ended the call but left his phone on the table. Jean, her hands now clean, opened the oven door and slid the casserole dish inside.

"Does she really think a potential relative would try to scam you right off the bat?" Jean asked.

"Who knows. She probably thinks Ancestry is the scammer."

"That's going to take about forty minutes or so to cook."

Jean got two plates out of the cabinet and set them on the counter before sitting down at the kitchen table.

"You want a drink?" Donald asked, jumping up and going to the fridge.

"Diet Coke."

Donald brought two cans of Diet Coke and sat down across from her.

"If this thing leads to finding your birth parents, you need to have patience with your mother," Jean said after they had each taken a drink.

"I know."

"She has raised you from a baby. She really is your mother, and I'm sure she feels threatened."

Donald nodded.

"And for God's sakes, don't ever refer to your biological parents as your real parents."

Donald nodded more emphatically. "I made that mistake once when I was a teenager. The look on her face was heartbreaking."

"So you know."

"Yeah." He looked over toward the oven. "Forty minutes, huh?"

"Yeah. Oh, before we forget." She jumped up and grabbed a Metformin pill from the bottle in the cabinet and set it on the table next to Donald's can of Diet Coke.

Donald sighed. "I feel like an old man having to take pills every meal."

"It's just one pill, and you don't have to take it every meal."

He picked the pill up and looked at it.

"Don't take it now. Wait until you've eaten."

"I know. Nag."

"Dork."

8

Donald had just returned to his desk after a lunch at Mi Cocina Mexican restaurant where he had selected a taco salad instead of his usual enchilada plate when he saw the notification from Ancestry.com in his personal email. "You have a new direct message," it said. Donald opened the browser on his office computer and logged into his Ancestry account. The message was from Barbara Janney.

Dear Donald and Jean: My daughter Nan got pregnant at seventeen and had planned on giving the baby up for adoption. Everything was ready to go, but there were complications during the birth. The baby had to go into the NICU for several days. By the time he got out, Nan had changed her mind and decided to keep the baby. This was on April 2, 1979 in Shreveport, which is really strange. This is from a DNA test? You don't think there could have been a mixup at the hospital, do you?

Donald read the message three times to try to make sense of it. The girl had decided to give her baby up for adoption and then changed her mind? And at the same time and place as his own birth? It didn't make sense. And according to Ancestry, he and this woman were related. She had to be his grandmother. If Nan was seventeen in 1979, she would be sixty now. Meaning that Barbara Janney would have to be approaching eighty if not already past it. Maybe she was misremembering.

49

DNA couldn't be wrong, could it? Shaking his head, Donald clicked on the Reply button.

Dear Barbara: Thanks for writing back so quickly. You said your daughter's name is Nan. That's interesting since my adoptive mother's name is Nancy. You said that your daughter wound up keeping her baby after a stint in the NICU. But my DNA test is conclusive that you are a close relative, either a grandmother or an aunt. Perhaps there actually was a mixup at the hospital. Were you present when your daughter had the baby? I'm just wondering if anyone who saw the baby in the delivery room had any question that the baby she took home was the same baby she gave birth to. Thanks, Donald

He looked at it, removed the word adoptive, and hit the send button. He then sent Jean a text telling her to look at the messages in the Ancestry account.

"Strange," she texted back after a few minutes.

Donald's afternoon was spent rebuilding the Chief Financial Officer's desktop computer after a hard drive crash, so he was too busy to check his personal email. The first thing he did when he got home was collect all the trash and recycling in the house, load it into the dumpsters in the garage, and pull those dumpsters to the curb. Jean pulled into the driveway as Donald walked back toward the open garage. He stopped at the concrete lip between the driveway and the garage floor and waited for her to park and get out of the car.

"Hey there," she said.

"Hi."

She walked over and kissed him.

"How was your day?"

"Busy. How was yours?"

She shrugged. "So-so."

"I was gassy all day."

"Me too."

"I think it was that Keto dish that did it," Donald said.

"I hope not. It tasted good."

"It did. That's why I ate too much of it."

"Go easy next time."

They turned and walked through the garage and into the

house.

"Any word from Barbara Janney?" Jean asked over the sound of the garage door lowering.

"Oh. I don't know. I've been too busy to check."

Donald pulled his phone out of his pocket and pulled up his email. There was an Ancestry notification of a new direct message that was three hours old.

"Yeah, she sent something."

Donald sat at their bedroom computer and logged into the Ancestry account. Jean stood behind him, removing her blouse and bra as she looked at the screen over his shoulder.

Dear Donald: I was living in Little Rock when Nan had the baby. She had dropped out of school and moved down to Shreveport to be with her boyfriend. I didn't see the baby until well after she had brought him home to that mess of an apartment she was living in. I spent a lot of time cleaning and babyproofing that place, let me tell you. As far as I know, no one ever questioned Nan or her boyfriend that the baby wasn't the one she had given birth to. Do you have a photo of yourself so I can see how much you look like Nan or Robert (her boyfriend and the baby's father)? Barbara

"Should I send her a photo?" Donald asked.

Jean shrugged. "Sure, why not."

Donald typed another message.

Dear Barbara: I will attach a recent photo of myself and Jean to this message. With the DNA match and the dates and location of my birth matching up, I feel that, somehow, you are my biological grandmother. If that's the case, I was wondering if you could help answer questions about my family medical history. I was recently diagnosed as pre-diabetic, and I was just wondering if anyone in your family had any issue with diabetes. I'd also be interested to learn about any other possible hereditary conditions (heart disease, etc.). I'd also love to know more about Nan, how she is doing and where she is. Thanks, Donald

"How does that sound?"

"Good, except that I think Nan might be deceased," Jean replied.

"What?"

Jean took the mouse and clicked so that Barbara Janney's public tree would open in a new browser tab. She pointed to the name Nancy Ann Janney, 1962 - 2007.

"That's got to be Nan," Jean said.

Donald thought of all the years he had wondered about the woman who had conceived him, carried him for nine months, given birth to him, and then put him up for adoption. He'd judged her, forgiven her, and judged her again more times than he could count. And he had always wondered what it would be like to meet her. Now he'd finally found her only to learn that he would never get to meet her and ask all the questions that had been filling his mind all his life.

"Oh shit," was all he could say.

Jean put her hand on his back and caressed him. "I'm sorry, sweetie."

Donald took a deep breath and changed the last sentence to just ask if Nan was still living or not. He hit the attachment icon and navigated to a six month old photo of him and Jean at her company's Christmas party, selected it, watched it upload, and hit the send button when it finished.

"There it is then," he said.

"Do you want to talk about it?"

Donald stood up and kissed his now unclothed wife. "No, I'm good."

He knew he wasn't good, of course, and he knew that Jean also knew he wasn't good. He took his own clothes off and went to the kitchen to pull the two ribeyes out of the fridge. Jean sat in the living room and turned on the television. Donald opened the package and set the steaks onto a plate then went outside and started the grill so that it would be good and hot by the time he got the steaks seasoned. It was a gas grill, so he only had to open the valve and hit the starter button to light it. The hot sun felt good on his bare shoulders although the concrete patio seemed to scorch his bare feet. When he went back inside, he stopped by the shoe rack beside the front door and put on his sandals.

"Hot foot?" Jean asked.

"Yeah."

She had started the latest episode of *The Wheel of Time* on

Prime, a show that she loved but that he'd had trouble getting into, probably because he had read the book series and took issue with all the changes that had been made in the TV adaptation. Before turning his attention to the steaks, Donald turned the oven on, grabbed two thick sweet potatoes from the fridge and wrapped them in foil. It seemed strange to him that sweet potatoes were healthier for him and his higher blood sugar than regular, supposedly non-sweet, potatoes, but his doctor had confirmed it when she had gone over a list of foods to avoid and their possible replacements. He put the wrapped sweet potatoes into the oven, seasoned the steaks, and took them out to the grill.

Jean paused the show so they could eat, with Donald savoring every bite of his juicy medium rare steak, thanking God that he could still eat protein. He and Jean talked about various topics, avoiding any speculation about his biological mother or the nightmare he'd had over the weekend.

After dinner, Jean cleaned the dishes while Donald went back into their bedroom to check the Ancestry site again. Barbara had left another reply. "That's not funny Randy," she had written.

"Who the hell is Randy?" Donald muttered.

He hit the reply button and typed, "Who is Randy?" and hit Send.

He called Jean into the bedroom who looked at the messages and said, "This just keeps getting weirder and weirder."

"I know. Woman is in her eighties. Maybe she's just not all there."

Jean left to finish the kitchen. Donald surfed the local news sites. He told himself that he was just keeping informed, but he was really looking for any new information on the murder victims, including anything about the girl he had seen in the dream he'd had at the trailer a few nights ago. There was a story about the body of a young woman found in a vacant lot south of Mansfield, Texas, but that body had not yet been identified. Donald did another search for Elena Robles and found the same set of stories but nothing new.

After watching a movie together, he and Jean were both feeling frisky and made love first on the floor in the living room and then on their bed. As usual of late, Jean enjoyed it much more than Donald did. Afterward, they lay together in silence, Donald staring at the ceiling and Jean drifting off into a satisfied slumber. Over the years he'd been having the nightmares, he'd never had a problem separating the pleasurable sex he had with Jean and the violent sexual imagery from those nightmares. But now, knowing that the victims in those dreams had been real people and that those images he saw were most likely accurate, he was having a problem focusing just on Jean. To get his mind off that, he returned to Nan, who had died in 2007 at only 45. Why had she died so young?   Would Barbara be able to tell him? Did she mix up her messages when she referred to this Randy person? Those questions kept spinning in his head, keeping him awake in spite of his weariness. The last time he checked his phone, it was 2:16 AM. He must have gone to sleep right afterward because the next thing he knew, his six AM alarm was blaring at him. Thursday was going to be a long day.

9

Jean's Thursday did not go as well as Wednesday which made her thankful that this was only a four day work week because of the holiday. She slogged through, not thinking about the Ancestry messages from Barbara Janney until she was on her way home. Donald's last message, "Who is Randy?" had gone unanswered by the time they both got ready for work that morning.

She tried calling Donald from the car, thinking that he should already be at the house, but he didn't answer. That wasn't like him, but she didn't think much of it until she saw the police car in the middle of the street at the beginning of their block. There would have been enough room to drive around the police car if not for the officer standing between the curb and his vehicle holding up his hand for her to stop.

She rolled her window down and said, "I live on this block."

"What's your address?"

Jean gave it to him, and his eyes seem to widen. "Wait here, please."

The officer stepped away and said something into the radio on his shoulder, but Jean couldn't make out what he said. She hit Donald's number on her car screen again, but it rang three times before the officer walked back to her. She hit disconnect before Donald's voicemail could pick up.

"Park at the curb right over there," the officer said, pointing. You'll have to walk from there. Special Agent Sloan will meet you in front of your house."

"Special Agent Sloan?"

The officer didn't answer; he only stepped back and waved her through. Jean, her hands shaking as she felt on the verge of a panic attack, parked her Prius where the officer had indicated. She burst out of the car, leaving her purse and bag inside, pausing only to make sure she had her keys in her hand, and ran toward her house, hitting the Lock button on her key fob a couple of times. Despite the desperate desire she felt to be home, she slowed as she neared their house, afraid of what she was going to find. The closer she got to the mass of police vehicles, red and blue lights flashing, the more obvious it became that her house was the center of their attention, and the greater her sense of dread increased.

Jean's first thought was that Donald had suffered some ailment or injury. With the number of vehicles here, it had to be serious, but as she glanced around, she didn't see any ambulance and no fire department or paramedic personnel. There was a large dark gray van in the midst of the police vehicles, with two people in scrubs walking toward it. Fearing that it was a coroner's vehicle, Jean's knees weakened, and she almost collapsed onto the concrete street.

"Mrs. White," said a tall man in a suit and tie and an immaculate close-cropped haircut. He stepped forward and gripped her elbow. "Are you all right?"

"What's happened?" she said.

"We need to talk about that."

She turned to look at the man and his somber demeanor.

"Where's my husband?"

"He's safe."

"He's safe? What does that mean? I want to see him. Now."

"In time. But first I'd like you to come with me to my office."

"Who are you?"

"I am FBI Special Agent Jeremy Sloan, Violent Crimes division."

Before Jean even realized it, she had been led to the passenger side of a black Lincoln Navigator. Agent Sloan opened the back door and guided Jean inside.

"Where are we going?"

"Nowhere right now, but to my office eventually. You'll be

comfortable here. The motor is running, so the A/C is on. Would you like a bottle of water or anything?"

"What I would like is to know what's going on here."

"We are executing a number of warrants right now. That's all I can tell you until we get to the office."

A uniformed police officer, a woman with a barrel shaped chest, opened the driver's door and slid into the seat behind the wheel.

"Officer Gonzalez will sit here with you until we're ready to go," Agent Sloan said.

"I would like to go into my own house," Jean said, her voice sounding distant even to herself.

"I apologize, but that's not going to be possible for a while." He started to shut the door but thought better of it and turned back to Jean. "One of the search warrants is for your car. Would you care to hand me the keys?"

"Search warrant? What for?"

Agent Sloan shook his head. "I'd rather not tell you that right now."

"Why not? Can I see the warrant?"

"I'd rather show it to you at my office, away from all of this." Agent Sloan waved his arm toward the van and the other police vehicles in front of her house.

Jean didn't know what to feel. Part of her was angry and indignant, but those feelings were overwhelmed by shock and confusion.

"The car keys?" Agent Sloan asked.

"What if I don't give you the keys?" she said, the idea just occurring to her.

Agent Sloan shrugged. "Then we'd have to break the windows. I'd rather not do that, and I know you'd rather I not do that."

Jean handed him her keys, too dumbfounded to protest further.

"Thank you." He shut the door and walked away. Jean gazed at the dark van blocking her view of her house, her home, then looked out the left window at the houses across the street. Of the four houses she could see, three of them had people gathered on the front porches watching the proceedings. They were her neighbors standing there, watching as she and Donald endured whatever horrible life changing event was going on. She sank a little in her seat, hoping the window tint would keep those neighbors from seeing her.

Special Agent Sloan had said he was from the violent crime division and that Donald was "safe". She could only assume that meant that he wasn't a victim of said violent crime, and if he wasn't a victim, they wanted him for something. It had to be the nightmares, of course, and his connecting them with the murder victims he'd seen on the news. Donald had talked too much about them to someone, and now investigators think he was involved. But whom would he have told? He didn't even tell Jean, his own wife, the details. And what little he had told her hadn't been much until he started connecting them to those photos of murder victims. The only other person he would have said anything to would have been the therapist Jean had sent him to. But she wouldn't have turned him in over his dreams, would she? They were still just dreams, unless he had told her something more about them, something that this therapist felt compelled to report.

"Oh my God," she said aloud, realizing that this was the only explanation that made any sense.

Officer Gonzalez looked at her in the rear-view mirror but didn't say anything. Jean realized that the officer appeared to be barrel chested because she was wearing a Kevlar vest under her uniform shirt. Did they think Jean herself was so dangerous that the person they placed over her had to wear a gun and a bullet proof vest? Did they think she was involved? At least she wasn't in handcuffs. She wondered if the vehicle door next to her was locked. Officer Gonzalez didn't look like she'd be very fast in all her gear. What would she do if she tried to open the door and get out of the car? Ultimately though, Jean didn't have the nerve to try such a thing. She decided to sit and wait and try to think things through.

What could Donald have said to that therapist that could have led to this misunderstanding? And that's what it had to be, a misunderstanding. Donald could no more have killed any of those women than she could have. And she realized that this entire scene was all her fault. He would never have gone to a therapist if she hadn't made the appointment for him.

Jean looked out at the neighbors again. The number of people on the front porches seemed to be growing. What was she going to say to them once this all got straightened out and everything went back to normal? It had to go back to normal, right? She went over and over in her mind what she would say, but nothing sounded adequate. Eventually, the driver's side door opened. Officer Gonzalez got out, and Agent Sloan took her place. Another man in a suit got into the passenger seat.

"Sorry about that," Sloan said as he buckled his seat belt. "I had to sign off on a lot of things."

"I can't go into my house? Where am I supposed to sleep tonight."

"I'll have someone take you home when we're done. Everyone will be clear by then."

"They're going to lock it up, right?"

"Oh yes. Don't worry about that."

"When will I get to see Donald? Where is he?"

Agent Sloan put the car into drive, and let it roll past all the other police vehicles. "That depends on a lot of things," he said in answer to the first question while ignoring the second. "We'll talk more about that when we get to the office. This is Agent Sam Blackman, by the way."

The man in the passenger seat turned, thin and black with short curly hair, and nodded to her. Jean ignored him as she saw two local TV news vans arriving on the scene just as the Lincoln was pulling away.

"Did you have to call *them*?"

"We didn't. They have people monitoring police radio traffic."

"Great."

She buckled her seat belt since they were now moving, leaned her head back, and closed her eyes for several moments. After she opened her eyes, she watched the traffic moving alongside the Lincoln. She caught Agent Sloan glancing at her in the rear-view mirror. Of course he would be watching her. He was trained to watch people.

Their route took them toward Downtown Dallas near the end of evening rush hour. Their pace wasn't as slow as Jean would have thought as most people were heading away from downtown.   Agent Sloan drove the Lincoln into an underground parking garage across the street from the old Federal Building.   Once they got parked, the two agents escorted her to an elevator and up to the fourth floor, both of them walking on either side of her.   They took her to a conference room and asked her to sit on one side of a long table.   Jean could see Dealey Plaza and the old Texas Schoolbook Depository building out the window.

"Would you like a bottle of water?" Agent Sloan asked.

"Please."

He went to one end of the room and retrieved three bottles of water from a mini fridge in the corner. Jean walked around the table and sat down, her back to the window. Agent Sloan sat across from her, with Agent Blackman next to him. Sloan set one of the waters in front of her. She grabbed it, twisted off the lid, and took a long gulp, only realizing just then how thirsty she had been.

"Must have been quite a shock to come home to that scene," Sloan said.

"Yes." Jean screwed the lid back onto the bottle and set it in front of her.

"Anything you want to tell me?"

"About what?"

"Anything. Your home, your husband, your marriage."

"Whatever you think my husband did, you have the wrong guy."

"What is it that we think he did?"

"Given the number of vehicles at my house, it's not jaywalking."

Sloan laughed and then looked intently into her eyes. "Mrs. White, how often do you and your husband sleep apart?"

"Rarely.   He had to go help with an office move in Jacksonville, like, three years ago. To move the servers and routers and stuff like that."

"So you've slept in the same bed with your husband every night for at least the last three years?"

"Yes."

"And you've never woken up in the middle of the night to find him gone?"

"Like to the bathroom?"

"No, I mean not in the house."

"No."

"Never?"

"Never."

Sloan sat silently as if waiting for Jean to admit she was either wrong or lying. Jean was determined to remain silent herself and not offer any more information. She could only wonder what Donald might be telling them about his dreams and the crazy idea that they included actual murder victims.

"Were you home all night on May 28th?"

"I don't know," she answered. "What day of the week was that?"

"It was a Saturday night."

"Then no. We were out near Decatur."

"What were you doing there?"

"Camping."

"Camping?"

"Yes. We have a travel trailer at a, um, an RV park there."

"And you spent the night there on that particular night?"

"Yes."

She looked over to Agent Blackman who appeared to be the note taker of this interview. He didn't look up at her.

"How many people can verify that?" Agent Sloan asked.

"Quite a few, I think. And we have to put in a code whenever we drive in and out of the gate, so I'm sure the office can pull that up."

"All right. We'll need the names of the people who can verify that you were there that night and, preferably, the next morning."

"Well, we're not supposed to just openly share the names of people who go there."

"Why not?"

"It's a— Well, it's a nudist resort."

"And?"

"A lot of people can't let it get out, publicly, that they go there. Some of them are teachers; some are police officers. You understand."

"I do. But you need to understand that we are trying to collect the facts regarding a murder case, multiple murder cases actually, and any kind of discretion needs to take a back a seat to that."

And there it was, what Jean had already reluctantly realized, that Donald was the suspect in a murder. "Look, I don't know what that therapist reported to you, but I can assure you that whatever it is has been totally blown out of proportion. Donald only went to see her one time."

"What therapist?" Agent Sloan asked.

Jean looked at him, perplexed. He honestly didn't know what she was talking about. "His therapist didn't contact you?"

"No."

"Then what is this about?"

Sloan and Blackman glanced at each other, and then Sloan looked back at her. "Mrs. White, your husband's DNA matches that found in connection with several recent murders in Texas and surrounding states."

10

Donald's Thursday had gone from normal to Twilight Zone as soon as he parked his car in his driveway. He hadn't even been able to walk to his front door before a fleet of both marked and unmarked police cars pulled up and stopped in front of his house. A voice over an amplified speaker told him to stop where he was and lie face down on the concrete walkway in front of his porch. He was frisked, handcuffed, and told that he was under arrest for murder, and taken to the back seat of a Dallas Sheriff's Department Suburban.

The ride downtown was an ordeal, sitting with his cuffed hands behind his back on a back seat covered in plastic. The two deputies in the front seat were silent during the entire trip, both of them ignoring the couple of questions that Donald asked, one about when he would get his phone call and another about where they were taking him. He could see the driver's grim expression in the rear-view mirror, almost as if he was having to work at restraining himself.

Donald's thoughts went back to the previous week when he'd seen the story about the body found at Holland Lake Park in Weatherford being identified as Elena Robles. For a time after he had seen that story, he had begun to wonder if he hadn't somehow committed the crimes he had seen in his dreams, with his conscious mind not allowing him to acknowledge them outside of those dreams, as crazy as that sounded. He had ruled that out for a whole host of reasons, but now that he had been arrested, he had to reconsider that possibility. The police obviously had some compelling evidence against him, or they wouldn't have called out an entire platoon to take him into custody and, he assumed, search his house and car.

But no, he couldn't think that way. Those were dreams. He couldn't physically have gotten out of bed, driven to wherever the victims were, raped and killed them, disposed of their bodies, and gone back home without Jean knowing about it. There would have been evidence that the two of them would have seen in the car and in their house. He would have tracked in mud or blood or something. There had never been anything like that, nothing to make him question whether he was committing any crime. Donald had to remember that when they started questioning him. He would admit to nothing and then try to hear what evidence they had.

The booking at the Lew Sterrett Justice Center, the official name of the Dallas County jail, was quick. Having never been arrested before, Donald was afraid of a full body cavity search, but they didn't do that. The search was, however, far more thorough than the frisking officers had done in front of his house. The police had taken his wallet, cell phone, keys, and loose change while he was still in his driveway, so there wasn't anything to check in at the jail. Jail personnel recorded his fingerprints, took a swab of his saliva, snapped his mug shot, and put him in a holding cell with two other men. One of them looked homeless with filthy clothes that reeked of urine and grime. The other was wearing a mechanic's smock with his name above the shirt pocket, Brad. Donald had no interest in talking to either one of them, but Brad sat close to him asked him what he had been arrested for.

"Murder," he replied.

"Well, fuck," Brad said and moved away from him.

The homeless guy didn't seem to be paying attention to either of them.

Donald sat silently and could only wonder what evidence the police had against him. He, of course, thought about his visit to Holland Lake Park last week while it was still apparently a crime scene, but how could that have led them to him? He could have been anyone just wanting to walk a trail in the park and hadn't seen the news. No, there had to be something else. Perhaps that therapist he had talked to had said something. If that was it, Donald thought that proving his innocence would be no big deal.

There were no windows in the holding cell and no clocks either, so Donald had no idea how long he sat there waiting. Eventually, one of the guards opened the door to the holding cell and called his name. He got up and found himself escorted by three guards into a small room with a table in the middle.

"Sit there," one of the guards said, motioning to a chair closest to him.

He sat down, and the door closed behind him. There was a mirror on the wall on the other side of the room, and Donald supposed it was two-way glass so people in the room next to this one could watch interrogations, like on those Law and Order shows that Jean liked to watch. He was left waiting in that room for a long time, although he couldn't guess how long. One hour? Two?

Eventually, the door to the room opened, and two men, one black and one white, both dressed in sharp looking suits, stepped into the room.

"Donald White," the white one said. He carried a manila file folder in his hand.

"Yes." Donald started to stand.

"Please, don't get up." The man motioned for him to remain seated.

The black guy had stationed himself on one side of the table and seemed ready to take action if Donald did anything abrupt. Donald sat down, and the first guy took the chair across the table from him, setting the folder on the table.

"Mr. White, I am Special Agent Jeremy Sloan of the Violent Crime Division of the Federal Bureau of Investigation." He motioned to the other guy standing at the side of the table. "This is Special Agent Sam Blackman. We have some questions for you, and I'm sure you probably have some questions for us."

"Are you related to Rolando Blackman?" Donald asked the other agent, although he couldn't say why. He was nervous and wanted to appear friendly to them, establish some kind of rapport. And maybe he just wanted to delay whatever was going to happen.

"No," Agent Blackman said.

"You must get that a lot, being here in Dallas."

Agent Blackman scowled and shook his head. "No, not really."

"Oh. Well, I guess it's been awhile since Rolando Blackman played." He had been a guard for the Dallas Mavericks in the eighties and early nineties, although his name and retired number still hung from a banner in the rafters of American Airlines Center. Donald's feeble attempt at light banter made him feel stupid.

Agent Sloan tapped on the manilla folder. "Let's talk about why you're here."

"Yes, why am I here?"

"First of all, I want to explain your rights to you. You have the right to remain silent. Anything you say can and will be used against you in court. And you have the right to an attorney. If you can't afford an attorney, one will be provided to you. Do you understand these rights?"

"Yes."

"And with these rights in mind, are you willing to talk to us?"

"Well, yeah. I'd like to know why you've dragged me here since I haven't done anything wrong."

"Good," Agent Sloan said as he opened the manila file folder. "Can you tell me where you were and what you did the night of Saturday May 28th?"

"If it was a Saturday, Jean and I would have been at our travel trailer."

Sloan looked down at a handwritten page in the folder. "At the Bluebonnet nudist resort, right?"

Donald was surprised Sloan knew that, but he tried to keep his expression neutral. "Yes."

"And what did you do that day?"

Donald shrugged. "Spent most of it in the pool playing water volleyball. Went to the trailer in the evening, put a broccoli and rice casserole in the oven, napped while it cooked, and took it up to the clubhouse for the potluck."

"And then what?"

"We cleaned up after dinner, took our dishes back to the

trailer, washed them, and went back up to the clubhouse for the dance."

"The dance?"

"Yeah, the club has a dance every Saturday night."

"How long does that last?"

"Until midnight."

"Did you stay until midnight?"

"Just about."

"Can anyone confirm that you were there until almost midnight?"

"Sure."

"Who?"

"Bob and Sandy for one. They are probably our best friends out there."

Sloan looked at his notes again and said, "Bob and Sandy McKinney?"

"If you already know this stuff, why are you asking me?"

"Just trying to get a clear picture." Sloan looked down at his notes again. "You slept that night in the travel trailer?"

"Yes."

"And you didn't go anywhere?"

"No, not until Sunday morning."

"Where did you go then?"

"To church."

"To church?"

"Yeah."

"You left a nudist colony to go to church?"

"They are not as incompatible as you might think."

"Where do you normally go to church?"

"Normally we go to Compass Church, but when we're out at the RV, we go somewhere in Decatur. I believe that morning we went to Crossroads Church there."

"Can anyone verify that?"

"It was our first time, so we filled out the visitor form. They should still have that."

Sloan looked over to Agent Blackman.

"Have you ever heard the name Elena Robles?" Blackman asked.

"Yeah, I've seen it in the news."

"But you never met her?"

Donald shook his head. "No."

"Never had any interaction of any kind with her?"

"No."

"She disappeared the evening of May 28th. Her body was found on June 18th but it took awhile for a positive ID. And then we had to notify the next of kin before we released that identification to the press. And yet, the day the story broke, you showed up at the site, trying to get into the park where her body was found. Seems suspicious given that it's such a long way from where you work and live."

Donald tried not to sigh. He looked from Agent Blackman to Agent Sloan who were both staring back at him intently. If he told them the truth about his nightmares, they wouldn't believe him. Telling was, therefore, a bad idea. However, telling them anything else would be a lie. These guys were professional interrogators. They'd spent their working lives detecting lies. Donald decided that the best thing for him to do was to tell the truth, bad idea or not. Maybe it would be a mistake, but he was confident that he had done nothing wrong. He'd had his doubts at one time, but those doubts had been erased.

"When I saw Elena Robles's picture on the news, I thought I recognized her from a dream I'd had."

"A dream?"

"A nightmare, really."

"So why did you go all the way out to Weatherford?"

Donald shrugged. "Curiosity. I wanted to see if anything about that place looked familiar."

"Did it?"

"No."

Agent Sloan sat in silence, just looking at him. Donald started to say something but stopped himself. In his situation, he didn't need to offer anything. And he somehow thought this stare down by Agent Sloan, with Agent Blackman looking on, was a test of some kind. So Donald just sat looking back at him.

"You recently submitted your DNA for analysis at a genealogy site," Sloan finally said.

"I did."

"Why did you do that?"

· "Because a test my doctor did about three months ago showed that I was pre-diabetic. When the doctor asked me if I had any family history of diabetes, I couldn't answer her. Because I was adopted as an infant. So, my wife had the idea of sending my DNA off to this thing to find out what we could about any hereditary conditions I might have to deal with."

"When you submitted that DNA, there was an option to make the results available to law enforcement. Why did you click that?"

"I didn't. My wife made the submission, and I think she clicked on anything that she thought would make a match more likely."

"If she had asked you, would you have allowed it?"

Donald shrugged. "Why not? I don't have anything to hide."

Agent Sloan closed the manila folder and took a deep breath. "DNA from that test came up as a match for DNA found on the person of Elena Robles after her murder. How do you explain that after just telling me that you had never met her or had any interaction with her?"

The stoic expression that Donald had tried to maintain vanished into one that he was sure expressed confusion and denial. He shook his head. "That can't be right."

"We also acquired DNA samples from your garbage. There were only two samples we discerned in that garbage, one female and one male. The male profile, yours, was also a match for the DNA found on Elena Robles's body. I'll ask you again, how do you explain that?"

"I don't have an explanation for that. There has to have been some kind of mistake."

Sloan sat back in his chair, not taking his eyes off Donald. "Why don't you tell me what really happened with you and Elena Robles?"

"Nothing. I never met her, never saw her."

"Where were you this past Saturday night, July second?"

"At the travel trailer."

"Can anyone confirm that you were there all night, besides your wife?"

Donald started to say no, of course not, but he stopped, remembering his late night walk to the hot tub. "Handyman

Bob."

"I'm sorry?"

"Jean had woken me up from another nightmare at four or five in the morning, and we went up to the hot tub around then. Handyman Bob came in while we were there."

"Handyman Bob. What's his full name?"

"I don't know. There are so many Bob's at the resort that they all have nicknames. But if you go out there on a weekend and ask for Handyman Bob, everyone will know who you're talking about."

"Another young woman went missing that night. We found her body recently and are awaiting forensic test results. We're not going to find your DNA on her person, are we?"

"I don't see how you could. I was willing to talk to you since I know I didn't do anything wrong. Whatever evidence you based your arrest on couldn't be accurate or reliable. But I'm thinking now that I may just want to talk to a lawyer."

"That's your right, but it means I can't help you with anything."

"I don't see how you're helping now."

Agent Sloan tapped the manila folder on the table several times. He looked over to Blackman who moved to the door.

"If you change your mind, just tell one of the guards that you want to talk to Agent Sloan."

He stood and left the room when someone outside opened the door for him. Blackman followed, and Donald was alone, feeling lost and confused. How could they have his DNA on a murder victim? That was impossible, and it didn't make any sense.

11

It had been a banner day in the life and career of Special Agent Jeremy Sloan. He had identified and arrested the suspect in what he had come to call, at least internally, The Tattoo Collector killings. Sloan was confident that Donald White had committed the rape and murder of Elena Robles. DNA evidence didn't lie after all. And if the DNA was a match for the killer of Elena Robles, then it was a match for at least twelve other killings (and probably more than that) in neighboring states. But something about Donald White didn't seem to match what he had expected. The identification of White as the suspect was certainly unorthodox and surprising. Sloan had resorted to forensic genetic genealogy, a technique used in cold cases over the past few years but not so often with active ones. He had hoped to find a close relative in the limited database available to law enforcement, a parent or a sibling perhaps, but was shocked when the perpetrator's own DNA came up.

A DNA profile had been created for the killer of Elena Robles which matched profiles in CODIS, the Combined DNA Index System, of other unsolved murders in several different southern and southwestern states. A psychological profile had been created based on those unsolved murders, one of a narcissistic sociopath, and White didn't seem to fit that profile. Sloan had only had a few minutes with White, but he was sure that if he had more time, those traits would show themselves.

Still, Sloan was going to do his due diligence. He'd already interviewed White's wife, just to make sure she hadn't been an accomplice, willing or coerced, in his crimes. Agents Taggart and Malone had been assigned to interview White's co-workers, his mother, and the people at the Bluebonnet nudist resort that he and Mrs. White had named. Sloan and Blackman would handle further interviews with Mrs. White and with the Whites' neighbors.

White's statement that he had dreamed of the murder of Elena Robles was unique in Sloan's experience. What surprised him the most was that White had told his wife about the dream ahead of time, before he knew he would be captured. Perhaps creating this dream persona was a way for him to deal with whatever remorse he might feel about what he'd done.

"He doesn't seem to fit the profile," Sam Blackman said on the way from Lew Sterrett back to the Federal Building, echoing his own thoughts.

"No, not on first impression."

"How many victims has he killed?"

"More than a dozen."

"You'd think some of that narcissism would show through."

"Yeah," Sloan said. "He must be a hell of an actor."

"They usually are. At least for awhile."

When they got back to the office, Mrs. White was still in the conference room where they'd left her. Sloan had promised her a video call with her husband, and he allowed her to use his laptop for that. Once that was done, he returned her keys and set her up with an Uber to take her home. Sam Blackman escorted her down to the pickup spot before going home himself while Sloan dove into the case file he had built. He checked his email and found a reply from Agent Hawkins of the Albuquerque office. She reconfirmed that the DNA profiles from four murder cases in New Mexico matched that found on Elena Robles, which, of course, matched that of both Donald White and of the previously unknown subject in CODIS. He checked the dates of those cases and found they were all within the last six months. That certainly did not fit with Mrs. White's statement that she and her husband had slept in the same bed every night for at least the past three years, but then nothing else about this case fit either.

Sloan replied to Hawkins's email, thanking her for the information and sharing the DNA profile from Elena Robles and the new Jane Doe case. He'd told White that they were still waiting on the forensic test results of the new case, but those had already come back. White hadn't seemed concerned about it, which was surprising to Sloan. Sloan was finding a lot of things surprising this week, not the least of which was the lack of any evidence found in the searches of the Whites' home and vehicles. Hopefully, a search of his workplace would be a little more fruitful.

Sloan checked the time, saw how late it was, and left to go to his apartment in Irving. Amanda, his girlfriend, who was a student at the University of Texas at Arlington and lived near the campus, called him during the drive.

"Hey babe," he said.

"Hi, how was your day?"

"Long, but good."

"How did the bust go?"

He'd had to cancel their dinner date for the evening because of the arrest of Donald White. Of course, he hadn't told who was being arrested or for what, but he'd had to tell her something to justify the cancellation.

"It went fine. Still a lot of things to clear up about it."

"OK. I have a final exam tomorrow and then classes start for the second summer session on Monday. Crazy schedule, right?"

"Yeah."

"But that means I'm free all weekend."

"How about Saturday night?" Sloan said. "I may be working late tomorrow."

"Sounds good."

They talked about various things for the rest of his drive home, and he ended the call while sitting in the parking spot outside his apartment. Once he disconnected, he went into his apartment, heated up last night's left over chicken parmigiana, and ate it in his living room, which was decorated with a few mementos from his short lived baseball career. He'd spent four years on his college baseball team and another six years playing pro ball. Sloan had never gotten past double-A though. He had been able to stay healthy, and he had worked hard. His problem had been at the plate. His best batting average had been in his third year, a paltry .243, good for a catcher maybe but not so great for an outfielder. When he left baseball, he found what he was good at, police work.

After dinner, he ran a hot bath. As he lay in the tub with his head resting against the back wall, one of his feet resting on top of the faucet, he finally figured out the biggest thing that was bothering him about the White case. In the few minutes that he had talked to him, White had seemed to be fairly intelligent. Why, then, would he have submitted his DNA for genealogical testing if he knew he had been leaving that DNA at different murder scenes? Forensic genetic genealogy had been used to apprehend rapists and murderers in several highly publicized cases since 2018 when it had been used to identify and arrest Joseph DeAngelo, more commonly known as the Golden State Killer. A widely publicized bestselling book had been written about the DeAngelo case, *I'll Be Gone in the Dark* by Michelle McNamara. And while the book had been written and published before the DNA breakthrough, an HBO documentary series had provided even more publicity. Even if White somehow knew nothing about the Golden State Killer case, forensic genetic genealogy had recently been used to identify and apprehend two Dallas area serial rapists from the 1980s and 90s, and those cases had been covered extensively by the local news stations.

Donald White, the owner of the previously unmatched DNA evidence, had to know this. He didn't commit his crimes in a vacuum. Why would he have willingly submitted his DNA to one of these genealogy databases? His story about his recent diagnosis and desire to learn more about his medical history from his birth family was a reasonable reason to submit for someone who wasn't a murderer. But White was a murderer. The DNA evidence proved it. The problem was, the DNA was the *only* evidence that proved it. Everything else ran counter to that, including White's submission of his DNA.

Actually, the DNA wasn't the only evidence, Sloan corrected himself. They still had proof that White had tried to go back to the Elena Robles crime scene. White had even admitted it. That was something, at least. And it was still early in the investigation. They were bound to uncover more.

Perhaps White wanted to get caught. He had created the construct of the dreams about the victims and shared that with his wife and therapist. He had returned to the site where he had dumped the body of Elena Robles. And he had submitted his DNA to a genealogical database. Why would he do those things if he wasn't feeling the guilt and remorse and wanted to lead investigators to him? But if he had wanted to get caught, why did he lawyer up instead of confessing to the crimes?

The water in the bathtub had cooled to something less than lukewarm by the time Sloan realized that he needed to stop thinking about the case for the rest of the night and get some rest. He pulled the plug on the drain, climbed out and dried off, and went to bed.

12

The FBI agents left Jean in the conference room while they went to the jail to talk to Donald. A couple of different administrative assistants would come check on her from time to time to make sure she had water to drink. One of them escorted her to the restroom the one time she needed to go.

Donald was a murderer. The notion still seemed impossible to her, but how could she argue with DNA evidence? The question that bothered her was, when would Donald have had time to do anything like this? Outside of working hours, they spent almost all their time together. And they even exchanged emails multiple times every day during those working hours. There was that one day last week when he had left early and left her emails to him unanswered. That had been such an aberration that it showed her just how much their lives had been intertwined, even for two people married to each other. So how could Donald have possibly done this? There was just no way he could have.

Jean didn't see them letting Donald out on bail with what he was accused of. And if they wouldn't let him out, all of the leg work for his defense would fall on her. And what if, ultimately, Donald wound up in prison? How would she cope? They had two car payments, a mortgage, and payments on the travel trailer. They didn't have kids, so they had been able to stay away from a revolving balance on any credit cards. She could sell one of the cars and get rid of that payment. The travel trailer could go too. She doubted she would be going out to Bluebonnet by herself. In fact, she'd probably avoid going any places that she and Donald had gone to together. How was she going to be able to handle the infamy of having been married to a murderer? How could her life have changed so drastically in less than an hour?

Jean hadn't wanted to call her parents. How could she tell them this? Still, they might see it on the news, so she had to get ahead of that. They lived in Houston, but this story might make the statewide or even national news, so she reluctantly picked up her phone. She called her dad rather than her mom, thinking he would be less emotional.

"Did he do it?" Dad asked after she told him about the arrest.

"I don't think so."

"They don't arrest people based on little evidence."

"No, they don't. But I don't see how Donald could have done any of this. We're together all the time."

"Not all the time."

"Well, we work, but outside of that…"

"I know from my Army experience that anyone is capable of the worst atrocities."

"Not Donald though. He wouldn't have."

"Well, we'll see."

Dad offered her support with whatever she needed and even offered to come up to the Dallas area that night. Jean was able to talk him out of that for the time being. After the call with her dad, she left a voicemail for her boss, telling him that she would be taking a PTO day tomorrow due to a family emergency. She thought of her friends, co-workers, and people at church, but she decided that she just couldn't call everyone. Besides, she and Donald hadn't been to a service at their regular church in two months because they hadn't skipped a warm weather weekend at the nudist resort.

The two FBI agents finally arrived back at the conference room.

"Well, can I see him now?" Jean asked before they could say a word to her.

"No, they won't let you see him, but you can do what they call a video visit," said the one who appeared to be the lead agent, Sloan she thought his name was.

He had brought a laptop and set it up on the table. Once he got the site loaded, he helped her create an account with her personal email address. When she got connected, Jean saw an empty chair in front of a blank wall.

'We'll leave you so you can talk," Agent Sloan said.

She figured the conversation would be recorded, but she appreciated the illusion of privacy. The two agents walked out of the room just as Donald, wearing a striped jail inmate uniform, appeared on her screen and sat in the chair.

"Jean!" he said, his voice sounding desperate and longing.

"Hi," she said back, not knowing what to say now that she could ask him anything.

"Can you call Vanessa in the morning and tell her I won't be in?"

"That's what you're worried about, telling your boss you won't make it to work?"

Donald shrugged. "I don't know what else to do. I don't know what's going on. I really don't."

Jean started to cry. "Donald, did you do this?"

"No. I didn't baby. I swear. I don't know why I had those dreams, but I know I didn't do this. I couldn't have. You know that. You *know* it."

"Yeah," she said, choking back a sob. "So what do we do now?"

"I need a lawyer. Someone who specializes in criminal defense. Can you do a search for one? I don't think we know anybody."

Jean nodded. "I'll look."

"Good."

They sat looking at each other through their screens. "How did this happen?" Jean asked.

"I don't know. They said my DNA from Ancestry matched what they found on the dead girl. I would think that Ancestry messed up, but they also said the DNA they found in our garbage matched it too. So, I don't know. I don't understand how this could have happened. But we'll figure it out. Just go find a lawyer, and we'll get to the bottom of it."

Jean found a tissue in her purse and blew her nose. "OK."

"I'm sorry."

"Me too," she said. "So, how is jail?"

"It sucks."

"Yeah. Dumb question, huh."

He shrugged and forced a smile. Looking off to his left, he said, "I have to go."

"That was quick."

"Yeah, I know. Just another way that jail sucks. Go ahead and schedule another video visit for tomorrow at 10:00, OK?"

"OK."

"I love you."

"I love you too."

Donald started to stand up, but the video cut off before she could see him finish getting to his feet. "Crap," she said and had to fight back tears. How were they supposed to be able to afford a decent lawyer?

Agent Blackman returned to the conference room less than a minute after the call ended, reinforcing Jean's belief that everything had been monitored. She used the computer there to schedule another call for tomorrow before she got up.

"We've arranged an Uber to take you home," he said.

She nodded silently, thinking that she might burst into tears if she tried to speak, and stood. Agent Blackman walked with her to the elevator and down to the ground floor. He even waited with her at the curb until the Uber stopped to pick her up, neither of them saying a word. The Uber gave her a polite greeting and asked how she was doing today.

"Been better," was all Jean could manage to say.

As the Uber driver left the curb and navigated through the Downtown Dallas streets toward a freeway, Jean realized the one person she should have called but hadn't: Donald's mother.

"Shit," she cursed under her breath.

She took her phone out and tried to compose herself enough to talk. She knew the Uber driver would hear her, but that couldn't be helped. This couldn't wait until she got home.

"Nancy?" Jean said after her mother-in-law had answered after three rings.

"Yes. Jean, how lovely to hear from you."

"I take it you haven't watched the news yet."

"No, I've been with my crochet club all afternoon. I just got home, in fact."

"Good. I'm afraid I have some shocking news."

"It's good that you have shocking news?"

Jean sighed. Talking with Nancy was such a chore. "No, it's good that you haven't watched the news because I have some shocking news. Donald's been arrested."

The line was silent for a long moment.

"Arrested for what?" Nancy finally said.

Jean felt the bile rising in her throat, and she gulped it back down. "Murder."

"If this is some kind of joke, it isn't very funny," she said after another silence.

"It's not a joke. It's…, ah. It's horrible. I'm on my way home now from the FBI office."

"The FBI? Why would they think Donny committed murder?"

"I don't know, but they found his DNA on the victims."

"Victims? Plural?"

"Yeah. There's several, they said."

Nancy was silent again. "This can't be. Not my Donny."

"I'm sorry Nancy." Jean felt like she would break down if she remained on the line with her. "I have to go. I'm sorry. I'll talk to you tomorrow."

Nancy started to say something else, but Jean hit the disconnect button before she could get anything out. Of course, Jean's phone rang almost immediately, with Nancy's name on the screen. She switched the phone to silent and dropped it into her purse. If Nancy wanted to know more, she could just go watch the news. Jean realized that may be callous, but she just couldn't talk out loud about it anymore. And she didn't want to have an emotional breakdown in the back of an Uber.

"Just pull into the driveway," she told the driver when they approached the house.

Both cars were in the driveway. Someone had moved hers from the curb where she had been told to park. That made her think that perhaps everything would be like it was before the search, but she was wrong. When she walked into the house, everything was a mess. All their Blu-rays and DVDs had been taken out of the racks and opened; the books from the living room bookcase were stacked on the floor; and the cushions from the sofa and love seat were leaning against the fireplace hearth. What had they been looking for?

She was too tired and hungry to worry about that now. The kitchen was a bigger mess than the living room, with items from the now empty pantry on the breakfast table and on the floor around it. Likewise, the pots and pans from the cabinet under the counter to the left of the stove were piled in the middle of the floor. At least food from the fridge and freezer had been put back in however haphazardly, and Jean couldn't help but notice that some large items, like the whole turkey and the ten pound package of hamburger meat, were absent from the freezer. Resisting the impulse to put everything back in order, she found one of the Lean Cuisine things she took for lunches and threw one into the microwave.

After eating, the first thing she had to do was compile a list of criminal defense attorneys to call in the morning, so she headed to the computer in the bedroom only to find that it had been confiscated. The monitor, keyboard, and mouse were all that remained on the desk.

"Great," she said.

She spent several minutes putting hers and Donald's clothes back in the correct drawers and making up the bed as the sheets had all been removed. It appeared as if the mattress and box spring had also been moved, but at least they'd had the courtesy to drop them back onto the bed frame. By the time she finished with the bed, she was too tired to do anything else. She got out of the clothes she was wearing and lay on the top sheet, searching for attorneys on her phone's browser. When she found a candidate, she left the page loaded and opened a new browser tab to search for another one. After about ten open tabs, she decided that was enough to start with, attached her phone to the charger, and turned out the light. As exhausted as she felt, she figured she would fall asleep right away, but she didn't. A mental picture of Donald strapped to a gurney in the state of Texas's execution chamber formed in her head. What if, God forbid, it came to that? Would she go? Could she watch her husband, her beloved, be put to death?

That couldn't happen, she decided, but the thoughts kept swirling in her head. She looked over at the spot where

Donald should be, empty now. Jean felt a chill, got out of bed long enough to slip under the top sheet. They kept the thermostat set on 78 in the summer to save on the electric bill. Because they were almost always nude at home anyway, they didn't need to blast the air conditioning. But her chills weren't from the temperature, and the sheet didn't make a difference.

After a while, Jean checked her phone screen and saw that she had been lying in bed for almost two hours. She thought about taking something, either a melatonin or something stronger. Then she thought of getting up and calling someone to come over so she wouldn't be alone. But who would she call? She thought about Brenda from church, the church she and Donald hadn't been to since early May. And she thought about Sandy from the resort. But Sandy lived in Weatherford, at least an hour's drive away. There was only one person she considered her best friend, and he was sitting in a jail cell in Dallas. Setting the phone down, she tried to sleep again. Eventually, she did.

13

Jeremy Sloan had at least a week's worth of work to do in one day. He started that by looking over reports while still at home. The body found outside Mansfield had been identified, and she was exactly who everyone thought she was. Sloan would be stopping by the girl's parents later that morning to deliver the news before any kind of announcement was made to the public. Most FBI agents would leave such difficult tasks to local law enforcement, but Sloan thought that hearing the news from him might give the family some solace, knowing that the FBI, and therefore the full weight of the federal government, was on the case. He hated delivering such news, anyone would, but he felt it was his duty. And doing so kept him grounded. It reminded him of the victims, the people hurt the most by these violent criminals, that his job meant much more than just a cat and mouse game with the suspects and the procedural gathering and cataloging of evidence.

After that, he had a scheduled call with Lawrence DeLuca, the assistant district attorney prosecuting Donald White. Later in the day, he planned on canvassing the Whites' neighbors and then conducting another interview of Mrs. White. He had a full agenda, unless something else came up, which it almost always seemed to do.

His first stop, he thought as he skimmed the reports on his laptop screen while shaving and brushing his teeth, would be White's workplace. The report on the computer at White's

83

residence revealed a recent browser history of several news stories about murders of young women around the region, not all of them attributable to him. Interestingly, that only started a week ago. There was nothing like that in his history older than a week, either deleted or otherwise. The most recent hit on any pornography site was over two years ago which certainly didn't fit with a sexual predator. The search and seizure from White's residence had turned up no physical evidence whatsoever connecting him to the murders. No weapons, no items that had belonged to the victims, and no other souvenirs from the killings had been found. It had been those souvenirs that had been at the top of this list of things they were looking for, mainly because finding those would have given them an idea of how many victims there had actually been, not to mention providing additional solid evidence, beyond that of the DNA, that White was the murderer.

Sloan spent less than five minutes in the shower, dressed in his regular Friday suit, and headed out. The drive to the Los Colinas office of White's employer was a short one for him. Sam Blackman, who lived in Plano, had a much longer drive and had given himself ample time in case there were any traffic tie-ups. There hadn't been that morning, and he was waiting for Sloan in front of the parking garage elevators at 7:55 AM, a Starbucks cup in his hand.

"Morning," Blackman said.

"Good morning," Sloan said, hitting the elevator call button. "Long day ahead."

"Yeah. Hopefully, we can wrap everything up though."

The elevator doors opened, and they rode up to the main level. No one was at the reception desk yet, so the two of them stood waiting until someone passing by in the hall saw them and stopped to ask them if they'd been helped. Sloan flashed his FBI badge and asked to see the director of Human Resources. The person scurried away, and Sam smirked at Sloan. They had talked on numerous occasions about the power of an FBI badge and how it instilled either reverence or fear in whoever sees it. He could imagine the lady whispering to everyone she saw along the way, "The FBI is here."

Less than two minutes later, a thin man with short hair that could almost be called a crew cut swept into the reception area.

"Hello, I'm Jeff Vance, the HR director here."

He extended his hand, and Sloan shook it automatically. "I'm Special Agent Jeremy Sloan of the FBI's Violent Crimes division. This is Special Agent Sam Blackman." The two of them shook hands. "We're here to talk about one of your employees, Donald White."

"Yes, I saw the news yesterday and anticipated someone coming today. How can we help?"

"We'd like to see his attendance records, when he took vacation or sick time, and take a look at his workspace and his computer. We have a warrant for all that."

Sloan handed the warrant to Vance who unfolded it and scanned the first page before giving it back.

"All right," Vance said. "I think we can accommodate that. Come on, I'll introduce you to his manager."

The two FBI agents followed the HR director through a maze of office corridors until they came to a large open space full of cubicles.

"This is our IT department where Mr. White worked," Vance said. He pointed to a corner office. "That's where his manager, Vanessa Sprong, sits, but it doesn't look like she's made it in yet." He guided them into the cubicles, the walls of which were only about three feet or so high so people could stand up and see each other. Vance motioned toward one of the corner cubicles. "This is where Donald White sat."

His workspace looked like all the others. The desktop was attached to the wall on one side and held up by a short stack of drawers. Sloan waited for Blackman to take several photos at varying distances with his phone and then pulled open the top drawer. He saw post-it note pads, pens, and a box of staples but nothing unusual. The second drawer housed an employee handbook and a test guide for a Microsoft certification test on Windows 10. In the largest drawer on bottom were several hanging file folders without much in them.

"Ah, here is Ms. Sprong now," Vance said.

A short athletic looking blonde approached them, a laptop bag slung over one shoulder and a puzzled expression on her face. "Good morning."

"Good morning," Sloan replied before Vance could speak. He flashed his badge as he said, "I am Special Agent Jeremy Sloan of the FBI's Violent Crimes division, and this is Special Agent Sam Blackman. I understand that you are Donald White's immediate supervisor."

"Yes, that's right."

"I'm sure you've heard by now that Mr. White was arrested last night."

"Yeah, I had four voicemails and six text messages from different people. You want to come to my office?"

"Sure."

Sloan looked at Blackman, nodding at him to continue searching White's workspace.

"Can we get logged into his computer?" he heard Blackman say to Vance as he followed Vanessa Sprong.

She unlocked her office, set her bag on the desk, and sat down to start logging into her computer. Sloan took the seat facing her desk.

"Does Mr. White work from home much?" he asked.

Vanessa shook her head. "Never."

"What about during Covid?"

"He was actually the only person in the department who came in to the office every day."

"Really?"

"Yeah. He doesn't like mixing work with home life, he tells me."

"Can anyone confirm that he was actually here and not working remotely?"

Vanessa seemed to think about that for a moment. "Jerry from building maintenance could. He was here every day as well. But I can pull up the login records. They would show whether he had logged into his desktop here or on a laptop somewhere else."

"He couldn't have logged into the desktop remotely?"

"He could have," Vanessa replied as she typed, "but our records would show that. We use biometrics for sign-ons in the office, so we'd know whether he used his password or the fingerprint reader on his keyboard." She looked up at him from her computer screen. "I just requested those reports for the last three years."

"Thank you. What about travel?"

She shook her head. "Not much. He went to Jacksonville, Florida back in 2019, I think. Yeah, it was before Covid, so it would have to have been 2019, right?"

"That was for an office relocation?" Sloan said, remembering what Mrs. White had told him.

"Yes, how did you know that?"

Sloan, seeing a chance to establish a good rapport, smiled and shrugged. "I'm with the FBI."

Vanessa smiled and then laughed. "OK."

"So no travel since 2019?"

"Right."

"Can I see his attendance records? When he was sick; when he took vacation, that sort of thing."

"Sure." She turned her monitor so Sloan could see it. "These are his PTO requests."

Sloan took a photo of the screen with his phone, but he could see three long stretches where he had taken time off, and a smattering of individual days.

"How about sick time?"

"We use PTO here, so sick time and vacation is lumped together. But I can only remember him being out sick one day in the last three years. And then there was last Friday. He came in but wasn't feeling well and left really early that morning."

"A week ago today?"

"Yeah, I guess it was."

Sloan remembered that that was the day White had tried to get into Holland Lake Park while it was still marked as a crime scene. It was also the day that his web searches on unsolved murders began.

"How is Donald White as an employee?" Sloan asked.

Vanessa shrugged. "He was good. Wasn't my best, but he wasn't my worst either. Competent, good customer service skills, knows his stuff. Just a bit unorganized."

"Did he get along with the other employees here? Or did he keep to himself?"

"He got along fine with everyone as far as I know."

"And he didn't seem to avoid issues that required contact with people?"

Vanessa shook her head. "No."

"How about conflicts? Did he try to avoid them, or did he seek to exacerbate them?"

Vanessa smiled and shrugged. "About the same as everyone else, I guess. He didn't have any major conflicts with anyone that I know of."

"Did he treat women any differently than men?"

"No, I don't think so. If he did, I never heard about it."

"No issues with sexual harassment or anything?"

"No, nothing like that. He seemed like a nice guy. I can't believe he did what he was arrested for."

Sloan smiled, thinking of so many case studies he had read, from Ted Bundy to Dennis Rader. "You'd be surprised by how often people say that about some of the worst offenders."

14

Jean had been lying fully awake for at least an hour before she finally got out of bed. Even though she was taking a sick day from work, she had to start calling lawyers. It was almost nine when she got up, so their offices ought to be open. After brushing her teeth, she grabbed a pen, a notepad, and her phone and pulled up her browser will all its open tabs. There was one law firm that advertised a flat rate for all felony defense cases rather than charging by the hour, so she started there. She still didn't feel like talking to anyone on the phone about this, so she used the chat feature they had on the page.

"How much would it cost to defend someone charged with capital murder?" she typed after filling in her name, email address, and phone number, wishing she had her computer as she hated punching keys on the tiny screen of her phone. She could go to the office and get her laptop, but she didn't think she could show her face there at the moment.

Someone named Asmee appeared on the other end of the chat and said, "One moment while I check on this."

Jean started to make a rude comment about Asmee's name to Donald before realizing that he wasn't there. Sighing, she waited a bit before typing, "I just need a ballpark figure of the cost."

Asmee replied, "I understand. Is this for you or someone else?"

"Someone else," Jean typed, thinking that if she were the

one charged with capital murder, she'd be in a cell and not on the web chatting with this person.

"Could I get the full name of the defendant?"

Jean sighed again and typed, "Donald Louis White."

"Thank you."

After another moment, Asmee typed, "Is the defendant in jail?"

"I just want to know how much," Jean said out loud, but she typed, "In jail."

About that time, her phone rang, the tone making her jump, gasp, and almost drop the phone. It was her manager at work. Jean sent the call to voice mail and then set the phone on silent.

"Could I get the defendant's phone number?" Asmee responded just as a text from Brenda, a friend from church, appeared at the bottom of the screen.

"OMG, Jean, I just saw the news. I don't believe it. Do you need anything?"

"He's in the Dallas County Jail, so whatever their phone number is," Jean replied to Asmee.

"I'm in shock at the moment," she wrote back to Brenda. "I don't need anything at the moment except a good lawyer."

The phone vibrated in her hand as she switched back to the law firm chat screen. Donald's mother was calling. Jean sent it to voice mail.

"Has he been arraigned yet?" Asmee wrote.

"I don't know. I don't think so."

Another text came through from Brenda. "James March is a lawyer."

Jean shook her head. She had already thought of him. "I don't think he does criminal law."

"So no bail amount has been set?" Asmee wrote.

"It's a capital murder case," Jean typed back. "I didn't think they would allow bail for such a crime." *Or it would be way too expensive to bail him out*, she thought to herself. "I just need to get an idea of how much a defense would cost," Jean wrote.

"That depends on whether the defendant wants to plead not guilty or is willing to accept a plea deal."

"He's pleading not guilty," Jean wrote back.

Another call hit her phone. This time, it was her mother. She sent that to voice mail too.

"We'd need copies of the defendant's tax returns for the last two years and a list of all his assets," Asmee wrote.

"Can't you just tell me how much it would be?" Jean wrote, exasperated now. "Or do you need to see how much he has so you can determine how much you're going to take from him?"

"We need to make sure of his ability to pay before we take the case."

"To pay what? All I want is a ballpark figure."

"Like I said," Asmee wrote, "it depends on a lot of things."

Jean felt like throwing the phone across the room. She closed the browser window without typing anything else. The next law firm's page appeared on the screen. She instead opened another screen and googled criminal attorney defense fees in Texas. There were a variety of pages that came up in the list, and she soon determined that most places would charge a $1500 retainer and about $350 to $400 per hour after that. What she didn't know was how many hours they'd have to put into the case. She'd heard of murder trials lasting over a week. And then there was all the other stuff: writing motions to the court, pre-trial hearings, investigation for the defense. Jean figured on hundreds of hours, all at $400 an hour. How could they possibly pay for that without going bankrupt. Donald did have $100,000 in his 401K, but that would be knocked down to $70,000 after all taxes and penalties for taking it out. And she figured she'd have to get a power of attorney to do anything with it. She also had about $70,000 in her own 401K, but, again, taxes and penalties would eat at that.

If whatever lawyer she hired actually won an acquittal, they'd have to start saving for retirement all over again. That was if Donald could even find a job after the notoriety of a murder trial. Something like this shouldn't happen to an innocent person. The thought that he might not be innocent crossed her mind again. What if his telling her about his dreams and then connecting it to the photo of a victim he had seen in a news story was his way of preparing her for his eventual arrest? What if he had, somehow, actually killed that girl? *No, I refuse to believe that.* But they had found his DNA on the victim. Surely, some of that DNA had come from semen inside the victim. DNA that matched Donald's. That seemed to prove that he had done the crime. It had certainly proven it to the FBI agents who had arrested him.

Her phone vibrated with another incoming text, this one from Sandy from the resort. "I don't believe the story I saw. Tell me it isn't true."

For a moment, Jean thought about typing that she didn't know. But instead, she typed, "It's not. Know any good lawyers?"

"I wish I did," Sandy typed back.

It was then that Jean noticed the time on her phone, almost ten o'clock, time for her video visit with Donald. She put a long t-shirt on just in case the video visits were recorded. The jailers didn't need to see a naked Jean talking to her suspected murderer husband. Jean connected to the site and logged in, flubbing the password the first time, hating that she had to do this on her phone with its small screen.

When she did get logged in, the video screen took such a long time to load that Jean was about to get up and reboot her wi-fi router. Jean stopped getting up when it did load, displaying the same empty chair and blank wall she had seen the day before, and she could only hope that the video would play cleanly when Donald sat down and started talking. He finally walked into the picture at 10:02 still wearing the striped jail inmate uniform.

"Hey babe," he said when he sat down.

"Hi. How are you holding up?"

Donald shook his head. "I don't know. I'm starting to question reality, you know."

"Yeah."

"How are you doing on the lawyer search?"

Jean shook her head. "I don't know. It's going to cost a fortune. I may have to cash out both our 401Ks. With no guarantee of success."

"I don't see that we have any choice. Public defenders are only good at cutting plea deals, which means I spend the rest of my life in prison for something I didn't do."

"Or we could spend everything we've ever made in our working lives, and you could still end up on death row."

"That's not going to—" Donald started to say, but Jean cut him off.

"How the hell did this happen? How did your DNA wind

up on that victim? And don't tell me that someone is setting you up? In the first place, why would anyone do that?"

"I never said anyone set me up."

"Then how did your DNA get there? What aren't you telling me Donald?"

"There's nothing I'm not telling you Jean. I don't know how that DNA got there. That is the honest truth. Are you doubting me?"

He looked to be on the edge of tears, but Jean couldn't lie to him. "I don't know. This can't just have happened. What did you do?"

Donald was shaking his head. "Baby, please don't do this. Don't leave me all alone. Everyone thinks I did this horrible thing, and I didn't."

Jean was crying now. She grabbed a tissue from the night stand and blew her nose. "I'm sorry. This is just all overwhelming."

"I know. Imagine how I feel."

Jean tried to give him a smile. The words "for better or worse" entered her mind. She and Donald had had so many good years, and now they were experiencing the worst she could imagine. She had to stand by him, now most of all.

"I do love you," she said. "I'm just not in a good state of mind right now."

"I love you too."

"I'll find a lawyer by the end of the day today. I won't worry about the money. We'll have to just trust God, that He has a plan."

"I hope He does," Donald said.

15

Once Sloan was finally back at the office, he planned to compare White's time off records to the cases in New Mexico. He and Blackman had been in separate cars, having gone straight to White's workplace, so he hadn't been able to sit in the passenger seat and look at what they'd gathered. From White's workplace, they had gone to the home of Patricia Garcia's parents, meeting up with a uniformed Dallas County Sheriff deputy there, to inform them that their daughter's remains had been found. Their reaction had been heartrending as so many scenes were, but Sloan and Blackman remained the ever stoic FBI agents. Sloan did tell them that they believed they had her killer in custody which gave them some small measure of comfort.

But Sloan was a little less certain they had her killer now than he had been then. On the way back to the office from the Garcia's, he had called Agent Melissa Taggart to get an update. She and Agent James Malone had gone to the nudist resort the Whites said they frequented.

"A search of their travel trailer didn't reveal anything. They only keep non-perishable food inside, and a few sheets and towels. Other than that, it was clean. It was hot as hell though. I guess they unplug the power when they're not there. This Bob and Sandy they mentioned weren't on site," she said. "The lady in the office said that they usually don't arrive until Friday evening if they come out for the weekend at all. And she said weekends after a holiday were normally slow. But Handyman Bob was there. Real name Robert Sadler. He confirmed that he saw both Mr. and Mrs. White in the hot tub at around 4:30 AM on Sunday the third of July."

The coroner had put Patricia Garcia's death at between midnight and five AM on that same date.

"And the lady also pulled up the gate records. The Whites' code was used to enter the park at 4:37 PM on Friday July first and to exit the park at 8:43 AM on Sunday July third. They re-entered the park, or at least their code was used to enter the park, at 12:56 PM on July third. And they exited again at 7:24 PM on that same day."

"And no one can drive out of that gate without a code?" Sloan asked.

"No. They have a generic code for visitors that changes every weekend, just so they can get out, or back in I guess."

"So anyone leaving could have used the generic code?"

"Yeah. But presumably, no one but the Whites know their personal code."

"How many generic codes were used?"

"Overnight July second to third? None."

"All right. Did you get contact information for Bob and Sandy?"

Melissa sighed. "No, the resort wouldn't give that out."

"That's all right. I didn't think they would. Thanks."

The first thing he did after sitting down and checking his messages was to compare the dates of the New Mexico cases with the work attendance and vacation schedule White's manager had printed for him. Nothing matched. Donald White was busy at work in Irving, Texas on the days that four different murders were committed in various locations throughout New Mexico. Sloan was triple checking this when his alarm dinged. It was time for his call with assistant DA Lawrence DeLuca.

"How does our case look?" DeLuca asked after the greetings and pleasantries were dispensed with.

'Well, the DNA swab taken from Donald White at the jail matched that found on the bodies of Elena Robles and Patricia Garcia. White's DNA also matches that found in connection with four other murders in New Mexico over the past six months. And one week ago, Donald White was recorded by a Parker County Sheriff's deputy trying to get into the crime scene where Elena Robles's body was found."

"All right," DeLuca prompted when Sloan stopped and remained quiet. "What else?"

"Nothing."

"Nothing? But that's enough, right. I mean, shit, the DNA ought to be enough all by itself."

Sloan took a deep breath. "I'm not so sure about that anymore."

"What? What's wrong, Jeremy?"

"Nothing else is falling into place like it's supposed to. We have gate records and witnesses that show White to have been at a nudist RV park outside of Decatur when both of our murders are supposed to have taken place. Company records show that White was in his office in Irving during the time that all four murders occurred in New Mexico."

"Is all that enough to establish a reasonable doubt?"

"You tell me, Larry."

"Shit.   You know I have to officially charge him by tomorrow."

"I know. The investigation is still ongoing. But I swear, it's almost like someone else with DNA that matches White's is out there doing this. But that can't be. Only eight billion people in the world and the chances of someone having the same DNA profile as someone else is one in seventy trillion. It's impossible."

"And you said White is an only child?"

"Yeah, but he's…". Sloan stopped, his mind working.

"He's what?"

"I'll have to call you back," Sloan said.

Without waiting for DeLuca to say anything else, Sloan disconnected the call and pulled up Melissa Taggart's contact page. Agent Taggart answered after the second ring.

"Where are you now?" Sloan asked.

"Eating lunch at a Panda Express in Decatur."

"Where are you going after that?"

"We were going to go see Donald White's mother."

"Scratch that. Text me the address. I'm going to talk to her myself."

"OK. What do you want us to do?"

"Go talk to White's neighbors. I'll probably head over there after I finish talking to the mother."

"What's going on?"

"I'm not sure yet."

"All right then. We'll go canvass White's neighbors then."

Sloan killed the call, locked his workstation, and grabbed the file folder of papers related to Donald White and walked out of the office. Sam Blackman had returned from checking White's work computer into evidence and gave Sloan a quizzical look. Sloan ignored it, realizing after he exited the parking garage in the Navigator that he should have had Blackman with him as their directive had been never to interview witnesses one on one. But Sloan's focus was on only one thing.

The drive to White's mother's house didn't take long as Sloan kept at 85 miles per hour most of the way. The house was small and old, built probably in the 1940s, on Birchman Avenue near the museum district of Fort Worth. Sloan parked on the curb and walked up to the front door, making sure that his suit jacket hid the service pistol strapped under his left arm.

The woman who answered the doorbell looked to be about seventy years old with gray shoulder-length hair that hung loose and a pair of glasses perched low on her nose. She wore a long house dress and pink socks.

"Yes?" she said after she had opened the front door, leaving the screen door closed.

Sloan held his badge up so she could see it through the glass part of the screen door.

"Mrs. White, my name is Jeremy Sloan. I'm a Special Agent with the FBI's Violent Crimes Division. May I come in and speak with you?"

Her expression grew cross, but she unlocked the screen door and opened it.

As Sloan stepped inside, Mrs. White said, "You want to talk about my son, don't you?"

"Yes."

She sighed and walked through the living room toward the kitchen, which was visible from the front door. Sloan followed her, noticing her crochet project on the couch in front of a television which was playing a soap opera, and sat when she motioned to the small breakfast table. She sat across from him, elbows on the table leaning toward him.

"I'm not going to say anything that will hurt my son."

"Mrs. White, I'm not after your son. I'm after the truth. But to get to the truth, I have to uncover a few more facts."

Mrs. White leaned back and said, "My name is Nancy."

"All right Nancy. My name is Jeremy."

"Jeremy. Nice name. What do you want to know?"

"I want you to tell me all the circumstances around Donald's adoption."

Nancy shrugged. "We went through an adoption agency, and it was a traditional closed adoption. So there's not much I know about anything."

"You don't know anything about Donald's biological mother?"

"If I did, that would have defeated the purpose of a closed adoption. It's better that way. The kids don't grow up conflicted between two sets of parents."

It was Sloan's turn to put his elbows on the table and lean forward.

"Nancy, this is very important. Was Donald a single birth?"

"A what?"

"A single birth. Or was he one of twins? Or triplets even?"

Nancy sighed and looked away, toward the refrigerator with its array of photos held onto it by magnets.

"It's very important," Sloan said after a long silence.

"I'm sorry," she said. "When you keep a secret so long, you tend to forget what the true story really was." She turned to look at Sloan again. "We were supposed to adopt both of them. And we were surprised when they only brought us one baby. Donald's brother had to go into the neonatal intensive care unit, they told us. Something about his umbilical cord. He had come up underweight and struggling to breathe. He might have to stay there two or three weeks, they told us. A month later, someone from the agency came to our house. We were afraid that she was going to tell us that Donald's brother had died. But instead, she told us that the birth mother had changed her mind. We were scared to death, of course. We had so fallen in love with Donald. Much to our relief, the lady said that the mother had already signed Donald away. But she was keeping the other baby. Well, our adoption wasn't final yet. We were so afraid someone was going to come take Donald from us. When all the paperwork was done and we were officially named as Donald's permanent parents, you wouldn't believe the weight that had been removed from us. We, my late husband and I, agreed to never speak of Donald's brother, either to each other and most especially to Donald." Nancy shrugged. "So we didn't. And I honestly hadn't thought of Donald's brother in over twenty years."

"But you know that the other twin was a boy?"

"That's what they said."

"I don't suppose you know whether the twins were fraternal or identical, do you?"

"No. That never even came up."

Sloan pushed his chair back and stood up.

"Thank you Nancy. You may have just helped Donald and everyone else involved in this case a great deal."

"That's all you needed to know?"

"Yes, for now." She didn't look in a hurry to get up, and Sloan had other places to go and people to see. "I'll show myself out."

16

After ending her video call with Donald, Jean showered and then got back on her phone. She made an appointment for 3:00 that afternoon with the William Masters law firm, what looked to be one of the most prestigious ones in the area. If they couldn't help her or if they felt wrong for the job, she had the addresses of several other firms still loaded in her browser. The trouble was, how would she know if they were wrong for Donald's defense? She had no clue what she was doing.

Jean then spent several hours answering texts and taking calls. She spoke to her mother, Sandy from Bluebonnet, Brenda from church, and several other people who had tried to call her. Talking about Donald and the arrest was exhausting, but she did it to hopefully slow down the calls and texts. At 1:30, she got up and styled her hair and then put on her red blouse and a checkered gray skirt. Just as she was about to walk out of the house, her doorbell rang. When she looked through the peephole, she was surprised to see one of the FBI agents from the day before.

"Yes?" Jean said after cracking the door open.

"Mrs. White? Could I have a quick word with you?"

"I was just about to leave for an appointment."

"This won't take long."

She had planned on giving herself plenty of time to get to the attorney's office, so she wasn't in a big hurry.

"All right."

Jean closed the door behind the agent and led him into the living room. "I'm sorry; I don't remember your name."

"Jeremy Sloan."

He handed her a card which she looked at and set on the coffee table as she sat down on the love seat. Agent Sloan sat on the sofa across from her.

"I just spoke to your mother-in-law," he began and then stopped. "Actually, let me start further back than that. We arrested your husband based on DNA evidence. His DNA matched that found on two murder victims in Texas and four in New Mexico."

"New Mexico?" Jean said. Sloan had told her that there had been murders in surrounding states, and Donald had talked about Arizona and New Mexico in the dreams he'd had. "Surely, you don't think Donald went to New Mexico without me knowing."

"What I think doesn't matter. My job is to document facts. Evidence. We had the DNA evidence which is convincing and a lot more reliable than eyewitness testimony. But the prosecutor always wants the strongest case possible. My job is to build that case. Normally, when we get a DNA match like this, we look to place the suspect at the scene through other evidence. But the evidence in your husband's case kept telling us the opposite over and over again. The two of you were at that nudist colony—" He paused to look at his notepad.

"It's a resort, Mr. Sloan," Jean interrupted. "They don't call them colonies anymore."

"Resort then. You were both at that nudist resort, Bluebonnet, while the two Texas murders were going on. The evidence found at the resort corroborates this. Not as strong as DNA evidence at the scene, but still, it conflicts with that DNA evidence. And your husband was at work in the office in Irving, Texas while the four murders were committed in New Mexico. Conflicting evidence. It was like someone else with the same DNA profile as your husband was committing these crimes. But the odds of two people having the same DNA profile are one in seventy trillion. That's almost ten thousand times the number of people on the entire planet. There's just no way two people could possibly have the same DNA profile. Unless they came from the same egg and sperm."

The FBI agent stopped, waiting for a response.

"The same egg and sperm?" Jean repeated.

"Yes. You told me Donald was adopted and had submitted his DNA to a genealogy company. That's where we found the match to our suspect's DNA. You said he was looking for family medical information."

"Yes."

"And you found a possible match to his birth family?"

"Yeah, someone named Barbara Janney. We exchanged a few messages with her, and she said her daughter had a baby the same day that Donald was born but that that baby hadn't been given up for adoption. We figured there may have been a mixup at the hospital with people taking home the wrong baby, but she stopped answering our messages when we sent her a picture of Donald. She said, 'That's not funny Randy,' or something like that."

"Randy?"

"Yes."

Jean started to get up and check their computer before she realized it wasn't there anymore. Instead, she took out her phone and logged into Donald's Ancestry account. She handed it over to Agent Sloan and let him read through the messages.

"Holy shit!" he said under his breath.

"What were you saying about the same egg and sperm?" Jean asked when it appeared that he had finished reading the message thread.

"Your husband has an identical twin brother."

"What?"

"Your mother-in-law confirmed it."

"Oh my God," Jean said as the realization hit her. "Do you think this twin is the suspect?"

"I don't *think* anything. I find and follow evidence. And the evidence is telling me that there are two people with your husband's DNA profile. The only way that is even remotely possible is that he has an identical twin, and the evidence I gathered from your mother-in-law corroborates that."

"She knew?"

"Yes."

"That bitch."

"It's not her fault."

"No, I mean for keeping it from Donald his whole life."

Agent Sloan shrugged. He looked back down at Jean's phone, still in his hand, and took several pictures of the screen with his own phone.

"Does this mean you'll let Donald out of jail."

"I'll have to talk to the assistant DA. Your husband's name was in the news. This is going to be embarrassing for the Bureau and for the DA's office. But worse than that, the perpetrator has probably seen both Donald's name and photo. He can find out where you live. We may need to place both of you in protective custody."

"I was just about to leave to go talk to a defense attorney. Should I still go?"

"That's up to you," Agent Sloan said as he handed her phone back to her. "I have never advised anyone to not get an attorney. Was there anything on this Barbara Janney's Ancestry account that indicated where she is now? She mentioned Little Rock and Shreveport in her messages."

Jean looked back at her phone and went back to Barbara's main page on the Ancestry site. "No, nothing."

"OK. I'll do a search when I get back to the office. I do need to call the assistant DA though."

He walked into the kitchen as he dialed the number. Jean felt a surge of hope spread through her. She had begun to doubt Donald's innocence just as the FBI agent had, apparently, begun to doubt his guilt.

"Larry, this is Jeremy," she heard the agent say. After a pause, he said, "I may have found an explanation for that."

Jean stood up and walked around her living room, full of nervous energy.

"No, I talked to the mother," Sloan said into his phone. "There was a twin that they were going to adopt, but the birth mother changed her mind. She was scared she'd lose the baby they had, and when they didn't, they never talked about it again." After another pause, she heard him say, "No, I don't think we should charge him."

Jean just about jumped out of her shoes at this.

"I know it will," Agent Sloan said, "but what are you going

to do?" After another pause, he said, "I'm headed there now."

Jean heard him say a few more things in closing, pausing to listen whenever this Larry person said anything, and then end the call.

"Mrs. White?" Agent Sloan walked back into the living room.

"Yes?"

"Is there somewhere you can go tonight? I'm not sure it's safe here."

"I mean, we could go to the trailer."

"No, I mean you. I don't know if your husband will be released tonight or not. I am going to go talk to him right now."

"I guess I could go by myself."

"All right, do it. If he's released, I'll bring him out there to you."

He started to walk out the front door but stopped and looked back at Jean.

"I apologize for all this. DNA evidence is usually ironclad, and we were trying to prevent anyone else getting hurt or killed."

"I know," she replied. "I understand, believe me."

Agent Sloan nodded to her and walked out the door.

17

"I'm sorry," Sloan said to Sam Blackman when he got back to the office.

He had seen the three missed calls from Sam on his phone, and he hadn't called him back.

"Everything OK?" Sam asked.

"Yeah. I had a breakthrough of sorts."

"A breakthrough or a breakdown?"

Sloan smiled and faked a laugh at him and sat at his workstation. He'd started to call the prosecutor again on the way back to the office but realized he needed a bit more information before he did that. A search of the name "Barbara Janney" returned just a few hits. The only one who fit the age range to be Donald White's grandmother was an 82-year-old living in Texarkana, Arkansas. He found a phone number for her and called her from his desk phone. Her caller ID should show the Federal Bureau of Investigation.

"Hello," a soft spoken female voice said after two rings.

"Could I speak to Barbara Janney?"

"Speaking."

"Ms. Janney, my name is Jeremy Sloan. I'm a Special Agent with the FBI, and I'd like to ask you a few questions if I may."

"Well, OK," she replied with a waver in her voice.

"Recently, someone named Donald White contacted you on your Ancestry account, is that correct?"

"You mean on my computer?"

"Yes, that's right."

"Well, yes. But it was my grandson playing games again."

"What makes you say that?"

"Because he sent a picture of himself."

"Mrs. Janney, that wasn't your grandson. Or at least, it's not the grandson you know."

"What are you talking about?"

"What do you know about your grandson's birth?"

"Well, it was difficult. Randy had to spend a couple of weeks in the NICU, but he came out fine."

"Were you there?"

"No, I didn't even know Nan was pregnant until she visited with the baby."

"Nan is your daughter?"

"Yes."

"Where is she?"

Sloan heard Mrs. Janney clear her throat. "She passed away. In 2007."

Shit, Sloan thought. "I'm sorry to hear that." He waited, hoping she would elaborate on how her daughter had died, but she remained silent.

"Do you know where your grandson is now?"

"Last I heard, he was in California."

"What's his name?"

"Randy."

"His full name."

"Randall Jacob Crum."

"Crum with a C or a K?" Sloan asked while writing the name on a notepad on his desk.

"A C."

"And his birthdate is April 2, 1979, right?"

"That's correct. How did you know that?"

"And what was your daughter's full name?"

"Nancy Ann Janney. That was her maiden name. She used Crum as her married name for a while but went back to Janney when she finally kicked Slim out."

"Slim was Randy's father?"

"Yes."

"And what was the date of your daughter's death?"

"Why do you need all this?"

Sloan smiled. It had taken her longer to stop answering automatically than it took most people. "It's for a murder investigation ma'am."

"For Nan's murder?"

Sloan sat up straighter. "I'm sorry?"

"Nan. My daughter. She was murdered."

Sloan started typing on his workstation even as he still talked to Mrs. Janney. "We're investigating several murders. I'll look and see if your daughter's is related to any of the others." His quick search returned a news report about the discovery of Nancy Janney's body in Bossier City, Louisiana on August 1, 2007. She had been decapitated and dismembered. Sloan made a note to contact an acquaintance of his, Captain Cheryl Mackey of the Bossier Parrish Sheriff's Department, about it. He opened a new browser tab, leaving the story about Nancy Janney where he could refer to it again, and started searching for Randall Jacob Crum.

"You don't think Randy is involved, do you?" Mrs. Janney asked in her meek, wavering voice.

"Was he ever a suspect in your daughter's death?"

"The police down there talked to him about it a couple of times, but that's all."

"All right. I'll look into the police reports. Thank you, Mrs. Janney. You've been very helpful."

"So that wasn't Randy who sent me that picture?"

"What? No, it wasn't. Your daughter gave birth to twins. She gave one up for adoption and kept the other one."

"Oh sweet Jesus. Are you sure? I think Nan would have told me that."

"Yes, I'm pretty sure."

Sloan ended the call before Mrs. Janney could ask anything else. He found a couple of arrests for Randall Jacob Crum, one for vandalism in Bossier City in 1994 when he would have been a juvenile and one for disorderly conduct in Marshall, Texas in 2006. He pulled up a report for the disorderly conduct charge and read what amounted to a peeping tom incident in an apartment complex at three in the morning. The mug shot from that arrest was like looking at a much younger Donald White. Sloan downloaded the report and the mug shot and forwarded it to Sam Blackman, asking him to find anything and everything on Randall Jacob Crum. He then emailed it to DeLuca and then called him on his cell phone.

"I just sent you an email," Sloan said after DeLuca answered. "Randall Jacob Crum. He is the identical twin brother to Donald White."

"I'm looking at it now. Holy shit, he looks just like him."

"Yep. I'm heading to Lew Sterrett now to see White," Sloan said as he headed down the stairs toward the parking garage.

"We're going to have a problem with the press if we release White."

"We'll just have to tell them we fucked up but that we fucked up in the interest of public safety not just to clear a case."

"Not that. I'm thinking about this Crum guy. You know he's watching."

Sloan stopped on the stairs. "So we'll say we're transferring White to an undisclosed location."

"OK. That's not going to work if White shows up at work on Monday."

"He won't. I'll have him stay at the travel trailer they have out in Decatur."

"Will he follow orders?"

Sloan resumed walking down the stairs. "I don't know. I hope so. I'll tell him it's for his own safety and that of his wife. But we don't have grounds to keep him in the jail anymore, do we? He hasn't been officially charged yet, right?"

"Right. I'll call the judge now. The release order should be ready within the hour."

"Thanks."

The drive to the Lew Sterrett Justice Center was only a few blocks. Sloan was inside the jail less than ten minutes after leaving his desk. He was shown into an interrogation room where he waited for jail personnel to bring Donald White.

"I don't have to talk to you," was the first thing White said when they brought him into the room. He was dressed in the striped jail inmate uniform and looked like he hadn't slept since the last time Sloan saw him, with bags under his bloodshot eyes.

"No, but you should listen to what I have to say."

White sat down across from him. Sloan nodded to the guard

to remove the shackles from White's wrists. When the guard left, Sloan and White stared at each other.

"There have been some developments in your case," Sloan said.

White remained silent, waiting. He was playing the lawyer card well.

"The DNA found at the scene of at least two murders in Texas and four in New Mexico does match your DNA. But I'm fairly certain it also matches that of someone else."

White's eyebrow raised. "Somebody else? Who?"

"I know this will be a shock to you. Your biological mother gave birth to identical twins. She gave one of them, you, up for adoption and was going to give the other one up too. But after a two week stay in the NICU, she decided to keep that one."

White stared at him with a dumbfounded look on his face. "Are you serious?" he finally said.

"Yes."

Sloan told him about the conversation with his mother and then with Barbara Janney. White listened without much comment, although he did shake his head when told that his mother knew about the twin and hadn't said anything about it in over forty years.

"So, the bottom line is, you're being released. Although we'd rather keep you in some sort of protective custody, but that will be up to you. Your wife is waiting for us at your travel trailer. I'd recommend staying there for several days, at least until we catch this guy. We know who he is now, so it shouldn't be very long."

Sloan thought there was so much White wanted to tell him but that he was holding back from a lack of trust. He figured it was still being in the striped jail fatigues and being in an interrogation room inside the jail that was making him clam up.

"Now, let's get you out of here," Sloan said and got up and knocked on the door. "You have his release order?" he asked the guard who opened the door.

"It just came in," he replied.

"Good. Get him processed out. He will be going with me."

Sloan waited near the outtake area the forty-five minutes it took to get White released. When White finally came out through the door, he had on the same clothes he had worn to work on Thursday, khaki trousers and blue polo shirt. Sloan led him to his vehicle and opened the back door.

"I don't get to sit up front?" White asked.

"After we get out of here. This is supposed to look like a transfer, not a release. Be lucky you're not wearing handcuffs."

18

Donald squinted in the late afternoon sunshine as the black Lincoln emerged from the underground parking area. Though he had only spent one night in the Dallas County jail, he felt as if he were emerging from a cocoon after a long hibernation. He was still reeling from everything Agent Sloan had told him, and he wasn't quite sure he believed it. How could his mother have kept such a gargantuan secret from him all these years? Donald also had to question the FBI agent's motives. He knew his rights and that he didn't have to say anything to anyone if he invoked his right to a lawyer, which he had done. Agent Sloan shouldn't have come to talk to him again, especially alone. Where was his silent partner anyway?

Almost as if in answer to this question, Agent Sloan's phone rang throughout the Lincoln. Sloan hit a button on his steering wheel.

"Hey Sam, you're on speaker. I have Donald White in the car with me."

"Gotcha. Last known address on Randall Jacob Crum is 1132 Jameson, Flagstaff, AZ which isn't even a real address. That's from 2019. His last income tax return was also from 2019. His employers that year were Maverick Foods, which operates several Wendy's franchises in the area, and AZ Rooter plumbing. His adjusted gross income for 2019 was only eighteen thousand and change. He's got the two arrests that you already saw. He's got an Arizona driver's license under that fake Flagstaff address which expires on April second of next year."

"His birthday," Sloan said.

"Yeah."

"No local addresses?"

"No, nothing yet. He's staying off grid."

"All right, thanks. Keep digging."

"Will do."

Agent Sloan ended the call. Donald saw him looking his way through the rear view mirror, but Donald remained silent. Sloan drove east, exiting in Grand Prairie and pulled up to a gas pump at a QuickTrip station.

"You can move to the front seat now," Sloan said before getting out to pump gas.

Donald tried to open the door, but it was locked. Sloan finished pumping gas then walked around and opened the door.

"Sorry, forgot it locks from the inside automatically."

"Yeah."

Donald got out and moved to the passenger front seat. Sloan got back in, and they resumed.

"I still don't get why you went to Holland Lake Park last week," Sloan finally said to break the silence.

Donald, who was still wary of saying anything that might be turned around on him, said, "I told you. I wanted to see if anything there looked familiar."

"Because of a dream?"

"Yes."

"How often do you have these dreams?"

"I don't know. Every month or two I guess. But it varies."

"These aren't normal nightmares, right?"

"Right."

"How so?"

Donald shrugged. "They seem real while they're happening. Not like regular dreams that don't seem real even while they're going on. And these dreams stay with me. You know how you forget your dreams not long after you have them?"

Sloan nodded. "Yeah."

"These aren't like that. I remember them like I remember

things that really happened."

"And in the dreams, you're the killer?"

Donald turned his head and looked out his window without answering. Sloan sighed.

"Look, this isn't an interrogation, and I've already told you that you're not a suspect any longer. I'm just curious."

"I am, but I'm not," Donald finally answered.

"What does that mean?"

"I see things through the killer's eyes, but I don't have any control over what's going on. Usually, in a dream, you make decisions, right? These aren't like that. It's like I'm aware of what's going on, but I don't have any control over it. I see myself doing these things, and I'm powerless to stop it." Donald had never put it in such words before, but he wanted to sound as benign as possible to the FBI agent. And it happened to be true.

"So tell me about the dream you had that led you to Holland Lake Park."

"I already have a therapist."

"Humor me."

Donald thought for a moment. "All right. Why not. When the dream starts, I'm driving. I can hear someone struggling in the back seat. When I glance back, I can see her lying there, hands and feet tied, a ball gag in her mouth. It's dark, so I can't really see where I'm going. I park somewhere where there are trees all around. I get out and throw the girl over my shoulder like a big sack of potatoes. I carry her down a trail through the woods, and then I drop her on the ground. I have this case or something on my belt, and I unzip it and pull out a pair of scissors. I use those to cut the girl's clothes off."

Donald stopped, not wanting to relate the rest.

"Go on," Sloan prompted.

"Remember, it's not me doing it. It's like I'm watching as someone else controls me. I could never do what he does in those dreams."

"Then use third person then. Like you just did then."

Donald paused for a moment, and almost laughed thinking about how the therapist, LeeAnn, had told him to use third person. "OK. He leaves her tied up naked, and he starts having sex with her. Raping her. She can't fight because her hands and feet are tied. And he times his climax with either cutting her throat or stabbing her in the chest with a knife he has in that case on his belt. It's all vivid and gory and awful."

"Is that when you wake up?"

Donald shrugged. "Sometimes."

Agent Sloan looked over at Donald several times as he spoke, long enough each time that Donald wanted to ask him to keep his eyes on the road.

"Just sometimes?" Sloan asked.

Donald didn't say anything, just nodded.

"Do you take… I mean, does he take anything from the victims before he leaves?"

Donald, of course, knew what he was talking about, and he didn't want to answer.

"Is this some kind of trick?" Donald asked after a moment.

"What do you mean?"

"You get me in the car, make me think I'm being released, no handcuffs." He raised his hands and put them back in his lap. "And then get me to admit to something that I couldn't know unless I had done this?"

Sloan shook his head. "No, absolutely not. I just want to know how accurate these dreams you have are."

"You actually believe the dream story?"

"Oddly enough, yes I do."

Donald looked at Agent Sloan, but he couldn't see his full face as he now had his focus fully on the freeway in front of him. "I find that hard to believe."

"You want to know why I believe it?"

"Sure."

"A few years ago, I saw this TV show about identical twins who had been separated at birth. It was part of some controversial study in the 1960s. I don't know if they purposefully separated them or it just happened like in your case. But they had a few subjects apparently. They found that the twins had remarkable, and unexplainable, similarities. Like one pair of twins smoking the same brand of cigarettes, driving the same make, model, and color car, taking their vacations at the same beach. But they each didn't know the other existed until they were well into adulthood. They'd marry people who looked alike, they liked and hated the same foods. It seemed like one pair even got the same tattoo in the same place. So I know twins have some kind of weird connection. I think you are witnessing the murders somehow, through some connection that I couldn't even begin to understand.

"Now it's true that we have withheld some evidence from the public so that we can determine whether someone has firsthand knowledge of the crime or not. So I ask you again, does he take anything from the victims?"

Donald took a deep breath. Did he trust this agent? Did he trust anybody? He had withheld that particular detail from the therapist just so he couldn't be implicated. But then, he didn't want to give Jean any of the gory details.

"After the girls are dead, he takes the knife and cuts off a tattoo."

Sloan swerved the Lincoln Navigator to the right shoulder and flipped the gear shift up into park. He leaned forward, looking straight into Donald's eyes.

"You saw that? In your dream?"

"Yeah."

"Did you see the tattoo taken from the last victim? Patricia Garcia?"

"No, Jean woke me up way early that night."

"That's right. How about the one before? Elena Robles?"

"Yeah. It was a skull with a snake coming out of it. I mentioned it to Jean, and she told me it was a Death Eater symbol from Harry Potter."

Donald heard the traffic whizzing by from where they sat on Interstate 30 between the Oakland and Beach Street exits. The Navigator shook whenever a tractor-trailer passed by.

"How many times have you had these dreams?" Sloan asked.

Donald thought for a moment. The dreams had started fourteen years earlier but had varied in frequency. Lately they had been every one to two months, but when they started out, they were only once every six to nine months. "I counted twenty-four not long ago, but there may have been more."

"And each one is unique? The girl is different; the place is different?"

"Yeah."

"Fuck."

"What?"

"At least twenty-four victims. Jesus."

"Over fourteen years," Donald said.

"Still, that's a lot."

Sloan slipped the Navigator back into gear and merged back onto the Interstate, heading west. "Is there anything in your dreams that might tell me more about him?"

Donald considered for a moment. "Like what?"

"You said you usually start in the car. What kind of car is it?"

"I don't know. I'm always inside the car."

"You said you remember these dreams like real life, right. You can't remember the logo on the steering wheel?"

Donald closed his eyes and tried to visualize what he saw in the last nightmare he had. The car in the dreams had seemed familiar to him, especially that symbol on the steering wheel.

"It's like mine," he said. "It's a Toyota."

"Is it a compact or something bigger?"

"It's about the same size as my Corolla."

"What color was it?"

Donald shook his head. "It's hard to tell since it's always nighttime. But it's dark. Either blue or black."

"Yours is blue," Sloan said.

"Yeah. You think his is?"

"It would fit with that whole twins story."

Donald shook his head, cringing at the thought that, short of appearance, he could be anything like the person who did the things he saw in his dreams.

<h1 style="text-align:center">19</h1>

Jean was a no-show for her appointment with the William Masters law firm. She didn't feel a need to call and cancel, but she didn't feel a need to go talk to them if Donald was no longer a suspect. When Agent Sloan left her house, she changed into something more casual, a pair of shorts and a Joan Jett and the Blackhearts concert t-shirt. The time she and Donald had spent at the naturist resort had made her a lot less caring of how the clothes she wore made her look. She left the house and went to her office, sneaking in the side entrance of the building, to get her laptop. A few people saw her, but she wasn't as concerned about that as she would have been if Donald were still a suspect. Carolyn, her closest co-worker, gasped when she saw her.

"Oh my God Jean, are you all right?"

"I've been better."

Carolyn walked alongside Jean all the way to her desk, peppering her with questions about Donald that she mostly ignored. Jean pulled her laptop off the docking station and shoved it into the bag that had been on the floor next to her desk.

"Do you need anything?" Carolyn asked.

"No, we'll be fine. Thanks though."

Jean slung the bag over one shoulder and peeked out of her office. She could see her manager's open door, feeling lucky that she didn't have to walk past it coming or going.

"I just came in for my laptop," she told Carolyn. "I gotta git."

"When are you coming back?"

"I don't know. There's so much going on now."

"If you need anything let me know."

Jean nodded to her and scurried away, ignoring the look of shock and surprise she got from her coworkers. Once out the door, she passed by a group of smokers. One of the guys from accounting, Sean, let his cigarette fall out of his mouth when he saw her.

"Jean?" somebody else said.

"In a hurry," Jean called back, realizing that she would still have to work with these people and couldn't ignore them outright.

The drive to the resort took an hour and a half during which time she fielded calls from her mother and Brenda from church, both of whom just wanted updates on how she was feeling and coping.

"Fine," she told both of them, wanting to get them off the phone as soon as possible.

They both asked if she'd talked to an attorney yet. She gave them the same one word answer, yes. After all, she had talked with the William Masters firm long enough to schedule an appointment. Jean also gave one word answers to most of the rest of their questions which must have given them both the hint, she thought, and made each call brief.

The trailer was hot and stuffy as it usually was upon first arrival. She immediately turned the power on to start the air conditioner, put water in the ice trays and set them in the freezer—she had forgotten to get a bag of ice on the way—and took her clothes off, as much out of habit as to try to keep cool in the hot trailer. She started to walk up to the pool area but stopped when she realized it was Friday. People coming in for the weekend. The pool wouldn't be as deserted as she hoped, and she wasn't in the mood to talk to anyone except Donald right now. So she turned on the TV and settled into Donald's chair which was right under the A/C vent.

The next thing she knew, she was startled awake by the sound of a vehicle pulling up right outside the trailer. She got up, looked out the door window, and saw Donald stepping out of a black Lincoln Navigator. Her stomach seemed to jump up into her throat, and the tears spilled out of her. She opened the door, burst out of the trailer, and wrapped herself around Donald, holding him in a bearhug. Donald held her just as tightly, and she noticed tears on his cheeks as well when she opened her eyes to look up at him. He kissed her before saying anything.

"I missed you," she finally said when he broke the kiss off to breathe.

"I was only gone one night."

"The longest night of my life."

He smiled the smile that she found so attractive when she first met him. "Yeah, mine too."

It was then that she noticed Agent Sloan, looking up at the sky, their trailer, his Lincoln Navigator, anywhere but at them as he stood there in his dark gray FBI suit.

"Thank you," Jean said to him, her arms still around Donald.

"Just doing my job," he replied, still not looking at her, and it was only then that Jean realized that she wasn't wearing a thing.

"Come on in," she said to both of them. "The trailer's cooled off now."

She led the way and found the robe she had worn to and from the hot tub back in April, before the Texas heat had taken hold, and slipped it on. Donald was right behind her, as close as he could get to her without tripping over her feet.

"Sorry about that," she said to Agent Sloan.

"No, no problem. This is your turf."

He stepped up and into the travel trailer, glancing around. One of the things Jean noticed about him was that he was always looking at his surroundings.

"It's nice," Sloan said when he caught Jean watching him.

"It's not much, but it does provide a nice weekend getaway." She motioned to the chair where she had just been napping. "Please, have a seat."

"I can't stay long. We've got several leads we are following now."

Sloan sat, and Donald and Jean settled into spots at the little dining table. Jean refused to let go of Donald's hand.

"I want you both to stay here for a few days," Agent Sloan said. "Donald, you need to keep out of sight as much as possible. If you need groceries, Jean you go alone. I don't want it getting out that Donald has been released. Right now, I'm not sure what our suspect is feeling. He's seen the news, and he's seen your photo. So he knows you look just like him. When he hears that DNA evidence led to the arrest, he'll put two an two together and realize you're an identical twin. We're going to be scanning public camera footage throughout the area, and I don't want footage of you skewing our results."

"Wait," Donald said. "I just thought of something. The Valero station just off I-30 in Fort Worth. It's on the access road right by Ridglea. I went in there the other day, and the clerk talked to me like I was a regular even though I had never been in there before."

"The other day?"

"Yeah. It was the fourth of July. Jean had taken a nap after we got home from here, and I went driving."

Sloan typed something into his phone. "If he's a regular there, then he either lives or works nearby. Good. You thought of that just now?"

"Well, you were concentrating on the dreams so much."

"Anything else you can think of to tell me?"

"No, not at the moment."

"OK, if you do, call me." Sloan handed him a business card. "My cell number is there, and I have it with me and turned on at all times. Also, if you have another one of those dreams, call me. Doesn't matter what time it is. Three in the morning, call me. Keep a notebook by your bed so you can write down any details you might remember right when you wake up."

"Wait," Jean said to Sloan. "Why are you so concerned about his dreams?"

"Because they aren't normal dreams," Donald replied. "Agent Sloan and I talked about this on the way here. Identical twins have this strange connection, and we think these things are visions into what he's actually doing."

"Like a psychic?"

Donald shrugged. "It would explain a lot."

"Everything about this case has been like something from the Twilight Zone," Sloan said, "so I'm not about to rule anything out."

He stood and straightened his suit. "I've got to go. Remember, you're lying low. Don't talk to anyone for a day or two. Unless we catch the guy before then. If you do tell anyone you're out of jail, limit it to close relatives and swear them to secrecy. OK?"

"Yeah," Donald said.

As Agent Sloan's Lincoln pulled away, Jean said, "Does he have the code to get out?"

"Yeah." He looked at her, kissed her again, and said, "I need to shower off this jail smell."

She looked over at the travel trailer's tiny bathroom. "I'd join you, but there isn't much room."

"Just be ready when I get out," he said with a wink.

20

He sees the woman from five houses away walk outside, get in her fancy looking car, back out of her driveway, and drive past him. He is already sitting low, but he leans over and ducks his head lower than the dash so she won't see him as she drives past his parked car. If she did see him, she would think he was her husband and probably stop. After waiting five minutes to make sure she doesn't come back for something she forgot, he gets out of his car and walks toward her house, trying to look casual.   The baseball cap and sunglasses help hide his appearance somewhat, but the people on this block are used to seeing his face. No, not his face but one just like it.

He doesn't want to be seen standing at the front door, so he tries the gate of the wooden fence on the side of the house. It's unlocked, so he slips in and walks around to the back door. Most of the door is a big glass window, but it's opaque. It takes him less than three minutes to pick the deadbolt lock. He walks in and gently closes the door behind him. He walks past the dining room and kitchen and into the living room. There is a framed photo on the fireplace mantle of the woman and a man who looks identical to himself. That would be this Donald White they arrested for the things that he had done. He picks the portrait up and studies the man and then the woman and then the man again. He wonders how he would have been if their places had been reversed. Would he have been like this man, living in a nice house in the suburbs, working a nine to five office job, married to a pretty wife? And would this man have been like him, traveling across the country, taking odd jobs that only paid cash and stealing to eat when he needed to?

He places the portrait back in the same spot. He's not wearing gloves, but he's not worried about leaving fingerprints. If they have the same DNA, they ought to have the same fingerprints unless he has any scars on his fingertips. Given the kind of pampered, privileged life the man has led, he doubts he has any such scars.

A car rolls by outside, slowing down, and he jumps to the front window to see if it's stopping. A garage door is opening across the street two houses down, and the car turns into that driveway. He turns and sees the master bedroom to his right. The room is neat and well kept, although the bed is unmade. When he walks in, he sees more photos of the man and the woman. These are smaller and are in frames lined up on top of the dresser. One is of them in front of the Arch in St. Louis. Another is of them at a baseball game with that same Arch in the background behind the outfield seats. He laughs at the third one he sees, the man and woman in front of a sign that says "Uranus Fudge Factory".

There is a picture on the wall of footprints in sand along with a poem about Jesus. There's also a painting that looks to be original of a small house in the middle of a field of corn stalks. He wonders if it's worth anything. There's a desk in the corner with a flat screen monitor, keyboard, and mouse but no computer. Ignoring the master bathroom and the closet, he wanders out and sees two other rooms on the other side of the living area. One is set up as an office with a monitor, keyboard, mouse, and empty docking station for a laptop. There is also a recliner with a box of yarn on the floor next to it. The other room is set up as a guest bedroom with a bed that is tidily made up. The chest of drawers in that room is empty. At least the two drawers he slides open are empty. He ignores the others. There is nothing under the bed, and with the frill on the bottom, he knows that a person could hide under there if necessary.

He walks back into the living room and sits on the sofa, staring at the portrait above the fireplace. It occurs to him that he could walk away, let the man in the photo go to prison for the things he has done. He could walk away, live a regular life. But he knows he can no longer ignore the pull of the hunt and the thrill of the taking any more than he can ignore breathing. That moment of possessing someone, making her his, is worth all the searching, stalking, and planning that he puts into it. He couldn't give that up. But what happens when they get a DNA sample from one that he does after the man is sent to prison? Then they'll know he couldn't have done it. He laughs at the thought of how perplexed they'd be. He was perplexed himself when he saw the story that the man had been arrested based on that DNA evidence. Until he figured it out. His mother had always said that she wished she'd given him away like she gave away his brother. Turns out, she wasn't lying after all.

He could alter what he does so that he doesn't leave DNA, but that would remove his reason for being. His release, their release. They both have to happen at the same time for any kind of satisfaction. Otherwise, why do it at all? And they'd find DNA from other sources. He couldn't clean all the hairs from the place, all the little fragments of him under their fingernails when they try to fight him at first. No, his only choice is to carry on as he has been doing.

He starts to get up from the sofa when his eye stops on a business card sitting on the coffee table in front of him. The FBI logo is prominent. The print next to it reads "Special Agent Jeremy Sloan, Violent Crimes Division". He picks it up, looking at the two phone numbers, one fax number, and email address below this. This, he realizes, is the lead hunter, the person in charge of the pack of law enforcement after him. He wonders if he shouldn't make the hunter the hunted. But no, the rest of them would be all over him if he did that. He wonders if this Jeremy Sloan has a woman, wonders if he couldn't take her from him and make her one of his. The thought makes him smile. He looks at the man and woman in the picture again, that man who looks just like him. The woman is smiling. She is pretty. Older but pretty. Not his normal type. But if she's good enough for the man, she'd be good enough for him. He wonders if he came here while she was here, pretended to be the man, how long it would take her to notice, to know that he wasn't the man.

He knows he's been here too long. He puts the business card in his shirt pocket and walks back through the kitchen and out the back door. He needs a key to lock the door from the outside, and he doesn't want to stand there with his tools picking the lock in reverse. So he leaves it unlocked and walks back the way he came, back to the car. Once he is sitting behind the wheel, he pulls the business card out of his shirt pocket and looks at the address of the FBI office in Dallas. He thinks he might take a look at it after he makes a stop at the public library to see what he can find out about Special Agent Jeremy Sloan on the computer.

<h1 style="text-align:center">21</h1>

On the way back to the office from the nudist resort (*not colony*), Sloan diverted to west Fort Worth and stopped at the Valero on the service road just off Ridglea Blvd. The fuel pumps were deserted. He pulled Donald White's mug shot up on his phone screen and walked in. Sloan was the only customer. The clerk sat behind the counter, a clear pane of plastic, installed after the advent of COVID, hanging from two chains between him and the rest of the store. The clerk seemed to take notice of him in his Friday suit and tie and sat up straighter. Sloan took a twenty ounce bottle of Diet Mountain Dew to the counter. As the clerk scanned the bottle, Sloan flashed his FBI ID and held his phone up to the plastic.

"Do you recognize this man?"

The clerk glanced at the phone screen and shrugged. "Yeah, he looks familiar."

Sloan glanced at the green digital number on the cash register, $2.17. He fished two ones and a quarter from his pocket and put it on the counter as he talked.

"Is he a regular?"

"Been in here a few times."

"When was the last time you saw him?"

The clerk shrugged again. "Three, four days ago."

"Do you remember what he was driving?"

"He usually walks here."

"He walks?"

"Yeah, I'm pretty sure."

Sloan took out one of the regular business cards, one with the FBI office's general number and not his cell phone, and handed it to the clerk. He thought about getting the footage from the security camera in the store, but they already know who the guy is and what the guy looks like. The tape might show what times he came into the store and what he'd been wearing, but it would take a lot of man-hours to find those visits.

"If you see him again, call this number immediately."

The clerk took the card, looked at it, and said, "Is he, like, dangerous?"

"Very."

The clerk picked the money up off the counter and keyed the amount into the register. The drawer popped open. He put the business card in the front slot of the drawer, where dollar coins would normally go, then made change and handed it to Sloan.

"OK," he said.

"Does the store have an email address where I can send this picture?"

The clerk recited an email address as Sloan typed it in, then emailed the photo.

"Print that out and post it back there for the other clerks to see, all right?"

"Yes sir," the clerk said.

Sloan pocketed his eight cents, took his Diet Mountain Dew, and returned to his Navigator. He looked around the tiny parking lot, the gas pumps, and the access road and Interstate 30 beyond.

"He walked," Sloan muttered to himself.

He thought about walking around a bit, but it was too hot to be walking around in a suit. Once he got into the Navigator and had his phone hooked up to the charging cord, he started the vehicle and called Sam.

"I think we need to concentrate our search in west Fort Worth," he said after Sam answered the phone.

"Why is that?"

Sloan told him about White's experience the previous week in the Valero and what the clerk told him about Crum walking there during his somewhat regular visits. As he talked, he drove around the area keeping an eye out for pedestrians and dark colored Toyota Corollas. He thought about telling Sam about White's dreams and about his "hunch" that Crum was driving a Corolla, but he ultimately decided to keep that to himself for now.

"There are a lot of older apartment complexes here. The kind that may not run credit checks. He's got to be using an alias since his name isn't coming up like we would expect."

"I'll call Fort Worth PD and check on any mobile surveillance video they might have in that area," Sam said. "The APB has been issued, so they should be cooperative."

"If he's walking, I don't think he would cross I-30. He'd walk somewhere on the side he's on. So have Fort Worth concentrate on the area just north of I-30 between Horne Street and Green Oaks Road."

"Got it."

As Sloan finished driving around the neighborhood, he and Sam talked about other things related to this case and to others. The good news was that the press hadn't yet caught wind of White's release or transfer. By the time Sloan got back to the office, almost everyone else had gone home. He sat at his workstation writing reports on the events of the day, transcribing a lot of it from his handwritten notes and composing the rest from memory. It was almost dark when he finished, and at this time of year, that meant it was around 8:30 PM.

On his drive home, he called Amanda.

"Hey, how did your finals go?" he asked when she answered.

"They went good, I think. Are you just now on your way home?"

"Yeah. It was a long day."

"You want to come over here?"

The thought of spending the evening with his girlfriend sounded infinitely better than going home to an empty apartment.

"I thought you'd never ask," he said. "Have you eaten?"

"Yeah, but that's all right."

"I was thinking about running through a Whataburger

drive-thru on my way there."

"Ooh, get me one of those Dr. Pepper shakes," she said.

"I'll do it."

Whataburger drive-thru's are generally slower than those of other fast-food chains since they don't start making burgers until they're ordered. Sloan used the time to check his email on his phone. Fort Worth PD has had an elevated CCTV unit at a strip shopping at I-30 and Green Oaks Road and was searching through their video. Sloan remembered the place. There's an Albertson's grocery store there along with a closed down BestBuy and a few other small stores, an Applebee's restaurant in front of the parking lot. If Crum lived nearby, and Sloan was betting he did, he has probably done a bit of grocery shopping at that Albertson's.

Sloan ordered a double meat Whataburger with a Diet Coke for himself and a regular Whataburger with a Dr. Pepper shake for Amanda. He skipped the fries—too many carbs—although he knew Amanda would berate him for it. When he got to Amanda's apartment, he was irritated to see that the blinds were wide open, and anyone could see everything in the lit-up living room. He knocked on the door, but it was Amanda's roommate Marcella who answered.

"Oh hi," she said. "Don't worry, I'm going out for awhile, so you two can have the living room if you want it."

"That's OK."

Sloan walked inside and looked out the window. All he saw was the blackness of the dark.

"How have you been, Marcella?"

"Oh, I've been OK. Taking the summer off from school, but, you know, still working at Starbuck's."

Sloan looked back at her and couldn't help but notice the flirtatious grin on Marcella's face and then the quick look away, almost as if she were blushing. She was a short Latina with shoulder length dark brown hair.

"Do you like working at Starbuck's?" he asked just to make conversation as he set the Whataburger bag and drink caddy on the kitchen counter.

"There are worse jobs."

"Yeah, I imagine there are."

They stood looking at each other over the bar, silent. They

both looked away for an awkward moment.

"Where *is* Amanda, by the way?" Sloan asked.

"Here I am," her voice came from the back.

She walked in from the back of the apartment, all 5 feet 11 inches of her, blonde, curvaceous, and beautiful. Sloan's breath caught every time he saw her, and even though she was just wearing jeans and a t-shirt, her hair and makeup were flawless. She walked over to him, and he kissed her, his hand in the small of her back.

"I thought I told you to close those blinds at night," Sloan said when the kiss ended.

"Oh, I forgot. I was making myself beautiful for you."

Amanda walked to the window and rolled the blinds shut. "There."

"All right," Marcella said, "I'm out of here. Don't wait up for me."

"We won't," Amanda replied, laughing.

As Marcella walked out the apartment door, Amanda looked into the Whataburger bag.

"Where are the fries?"

"I didn't get any fries."

"Why not? How am I supposed to dip my fries in my Dr. Pepper shake if there aren't any fries?"

"That, my dear, is a misuse of a perfectly good Dr. Pepper shake."

He grabbed her and pulled her toward him, brushing her hair back from her face with his fingers.

"Are we going to watch a movie or do something else?" Amanda asked.

"I'm voting for something else. After I eat my burger though. I'm starved."

22

It didn't take long for Jean to come up with a list of things they would need for their weekend in the trailer. Donald added a couple of items of his own to that list. So at about seven PM, she dressed and got in her car and headed toward the Walmart in Decatur. They both hated to be apart for even a minute given the experience of the last day and a half, but they both thought it best that Donald remain away from the public. Once Jean left, the first thing Donald thought to do was call his mother, both to tell her he was out of jail and to talk about the secret she had kept so long. But his phone was still in the possession of either the FBI or some other law enforcement agency, so he logged onto the laptop Jean had retrieved from her office. He tried connecting to the resort Wi-Fi which didn't always work in the trailer. But today it did, although it was painfully slow. Donald logged into his social media accounts. The number of comments and messages he had received since his arrest was overwhelming, so he logged out of those and into his Ancestry account. The last message he had sent to Barbara Janney, "Who is Randy?" was still there, but there was a new reply from her.

Dear Donald: I apologize for my last message. My grandson, Randy, has a history of messing with people, sometimes not in a nice way. When I saw your photo, I thought it was him. The two of you look that much alike. An FBI agent called me earlier today and told me that my daughter had twins and for some reason had given one up for adoption and kept the other. I don't understand that. I guess I never will. My daughter — your mother, I guess — was killed 15 years ago. Her name was Nancy, but everyone called her Nan. Nancy Ann Janney, although she was Nancy Ann Crum for awhile.

In answer to your questions, my husband, Richard Janney, your grandfather, had type 2 diabetes for the last eight years of his life. He also had high cholesterol and high blood pressure, but it was rectal cancer that got him in the end. Oh my, that sounds wrong, doesn't it. In the end. I'm sorry. It's been eight years, and I still miss him. He had that kind of sense of humor. His father died of a heart attack in 1977. His mother caught pneumonia and died in 1984. I'm not sure if they had any chronic conditions before that. My father died in World War II, and my mother lived to be 106. She died just last year.

I don't know much about your biological father's family. He was married to Nan only a short time. I think she kept the baby to get him to marry her, and then she used the child to get child support from him when they split up. I never did understand that girl. She had a lot of problems. Anyway, I hope this helps.

Barbara

Donald read the message twice before typing a response. "Thanks for that information. I take heart in the fact that my great grandmother lived such a long life. I do have to ask though, how did—" He thought about typing "my mother", but his mom was still his mother. Instead he typed "your daughter die?" to finish the question. He then typed his first name and hit send.

It was almost dark by the time Jean got back with the groceries. He started to walk out and help her bring them in, but she shooed him back into the trailer.

"Agent Sloan said to lay low and that's exactly what you're going to do. Besides, there's not that much anyway."

She got them all inside in one load, five plastic bags full. Donald did put everything up while Jean put a small Mexican lasagna in the oven to eat for dinner. They had just sat down to eat on paper plates and with plastic forks when they heard a knock on the trailer door. Jean got up to answer it.

"Hey there," Donald heard Baldy Bob say.

"Hi," Jean replied.

"We were heading up to the clubhouse for karaoke, saw your car, and wondered if you wanted a ride," Sandy said.

"Actually, I'm just going to chill here at the trailer."

"What! No karaoke?" Bob said.

"You have to keep on living," Sandy said.

Donald saw her eyes light on him as she looked past Jean into the trailer.

"Oh my God! Don, you're out?"

Donald stood up and went to the door to stand next to Jean.

"Yeah, it's long story."

"Come on in," Jean said, obviously nervous that others might see Donald standing there.

Sandy and Bob stepped into the trailer, and Jean shut the door.

"We were just starting dinner," Jean said, sitting back down.

Donald sat down at his plate and motioned for Sandy and Bob to sit next to them at what passed for a dining room table in the tiny travel trailer. They were both nude and their towels were out on their golf cart, so they hesitated.

"Just use our towels," Donald said, spreading the one he was using so that it covered the entire bench. Jean did the same, and the other couple sat down.

"I thought I saw that bail was set at a million dollars," Bob said. "How in the hell could you afford that?"

"We can't," Donald replied.

Jean told them about the lack of evidence beyond the DNA and how further investigation had revealed that Donald had an identical twin.

"That's crazy," Bob said. "It's like something you see on *60 Minutes* or something."

"Or *Ripley's Believe it or Not*," Sandy added.

"I know. I'm still trying to wrap my head around it," Donald said between bites of Mexican lasagna which was more like a tortilla casserole.

"But don't tell anyone else Donald is here. The agent told us he has to lay low. They're not announcing his release because they don't want the brother to know yet."

"All right," Bob said.

"So a real FBI agent brought you here and everything?"

Sandy said.

Donald nodded. "He did."

Once Bob and Sandy had left to go to the clubhouse, Donald said, "Do you think they'll keep quiet?"

"Bob will. I'm not so sure about Sandy."

"Well, I can't hide out forever."

Donald finished his dinner ahead of Jean, so he took her cell phone and called his mother. She answered on the first ring.

"Jean?"

"No, it's me, Mom."

"Oh thank heaven! You're out of jail, right?"

Donald smiled, winking at Jean. "Yeah, I am."

"Wonderful. I'm so glad that Agent Sloan was on the case."

"Yeah, me too."

After an awkward moment of silence, Donald said, "So, about what you told Agent Sloan…"

"Honestly, I haven't thought of him, your twin, in over thirty years. I mean, I never expected you to find anything about your birth mother, so we just didn't bring it up anymore."

"And you didn't put up any kind of fight to adopt him?"

"No! We were afraid if we did we'd lose you too. Your father and I, God rest his soul, got to take you home from the hospital, but it took about a month for the adoption to be final. Before it was final, we thought anything could happen. So we kept our mouths shut."

Donald thought about his parents as a young couple who couldn't conceive a child finally getting a chance to adopt a newborn and suddenly fearful that the newborn they'd just taken into their home would be taken away.

"Donny, are you mad?"

"Huh?" he said and realized he'd been quiet on the line for longer than he'd intended. "No, I'm not mad. I'm too tired to be mad at anyone."

They were silent for a moment before his mother said in a voice that sounded like she might cry, "Now I keep wondering what kind of life that other baby led and if that life led him to where he is now. *What* he is now."

"Who can say?" Donald said.

They talked for a few minutes, his mother apologizing a few

more times, before ending the call. After Jean finished eating, they lay on the bed holding each other which soon led to other more intimate things as they were already nude to begin with.

Donald hadn't slept much during his one night in the jail cell, and he fell asleep before he was even able to catch his breath, the pad and pen Jean had just bought at Walmart on the bedside table next to him.

23

He sits in his car for an hour watching the vehicles roll out of the parking garage and passing under a bright street light. He has to get out once to feed the parking meter. Don't want to get a ticket while he's sitting in the car where the parking enforcement officer can see him. The baseball cap and sunglasses can only hide so much. And it's almost too dark for sunglasses anyway. After his library research, he knows who he's looking for, and he finally spots him in a black Lincoln Navigator at 8:37 PM. Working late, trying to pin everything on that sap hopefully. He starts the car engine and pulls onto the street two cars behind the Navigator.

This is reckless and bold, he knows. He tells himself he just wants to see where this guy lives, the guy who has been pursuing him and wound up with his twin. Most people in his position would be keeping far away from such a person. But he's not most people, and very few are ever in his position. Besides, he's gotten this far, so he feels charmed somehow.

The Lincoln passes under the famous triple overpass, taking the same route that the car carrying John F. Kennedy with half his skull blown apart took almost 60 years before and makes its way to Interstate 35E heading north. He stays three to four car lengths behind, but he never loses sight of the Lincoln. At the Highway 183 split, it takes 183 and then exits at O'Connor. No one between them takes that exit, so he's right behind the Lincoln at the light waiting to turn right on O'Connor, but that's all right. He's been far enough back that he can be right behind him for a little while. The good news is that the guy wouldn't expect to be followed, so he won't be checking his tail anyway. The guy is used to being the hunter, not the hunted. When the light turns green, he goes straight and then, surprisingly, gets back on the freeway. He then takes the Highway 360 exit, heading south. This makes no sense. Maybe the guy has figured out he's being followed and is trying to lose him.

He stays four or more cars behind. The Lincoln Navigator is large enough that he can see it over most other vehicles. He follows the Navigator on Interstate 30 heading west to the Collins exit. After turning right on Collins, with at least two cars between him and the Lincoln at all times, he sees the Lincoln turn left into a Whataburger. He passes the Whataburger and takes a left at the cross street. There is another entrance to the Whataburger parking lot on the left, and he turns into it, backing into a space where he can see the Lincoln waiting in the drive-thru line. He turns off his headlights and starts to relax a little. Maybe the guy didn't realize he was being followed after all. The guy gets his order from the window and turns right onto Collins. That makes it easier to follow him than turning left would have. He turns on the lights and slips his car into drive. He follows the Lincoln past a university campus and into an apartment complex close by. He switches off the car lights as he turns into the complex a little after it. The Navigator parks, and the guy steps out, carrying his Whataburger order with him. The guy knocks on a door and is let inside. He inches the car forward, looking into the big window of the apartment the guy went into. When he sees the girl who had let him in, his stomach burns. She is perfect. Beautiful skin, hair, smile. He wants her immediately. But that isn't why he is here. He just wants to know where the guy lives, what his life is like. He stops the car, staring into the apartment as a tall blonde walks into the room. The guy kisses the blonde while ignoring the first girl. The kiss ends, and the guy says something to the blonde. She then walks over and closes the blinds, blocking his view into the apartment.

He parks the car where he can see the door the guy had gone into, which is good since the girl walks out of it just a few minutes later. She skips down the walkway and hops into a blue Volkswagen Beetle. The Beetle backs out and pulls out onto the street, and he follows right behind her, his lights still off. This is foolhardy, he knows, but he also knows that he will make her one of his.

The Beetle stops at a red light with his car right behind it. He looks up at the traffic light, sees the camera sitting there above them. He wonders if the camera works and assumes they use whatever footage there was for accident investigations. The light turns green, and the Beetle takes off. He lets a car get between him and the Beetle so he can turn his lights on without the girl noticing. Didn't want to get stopped for not having headlights on. The car between them changes lanes, and he speeds up and gets right behind the Beetle again. That familiar tingling has started in his chest, his breathing is quicker. He almost can't wait, but he also tells himself that he has to be careful.

The Beetle's left blinker comes on, and it veers into a turn lane that leads into a strip shopping center. He doesn't know where he is, but that doesn't matter. There's no camera that he can see overlooking this spot. He drives into the turn lane and bumps into the back of the Beetle, not hard, but hard enough to give the girl a jolt. After taking a glance in the mirror to make sure his expression looked right, he jumps out of the car and rushes forward.

"Oh my gosh," he says as the girl gets out of the Beetle, "I don't know what happened. I went to step on the brake and my foot just missed the pedal."

She looks at the back bumper of the Beetle. The bumper is pushed in a bit.

"Shit," she says.

"I have insurance. Come on, I'll get it and you can take a picture of it with your phone."

He walks back to his car, motioning for the girl to follow him. She finally does, and he waits for her by the side of his car. Other vehicles are buzzing past, and he hopes that none of them decide to stop and offer aid. He opens the rear left door.

"Here," he says.

"Why is your insurance in the back seat?" she asks.

He just smiles at her. When she's close enough, he grabs her by the shoulders and bashes her head into the side of the roof of his car. She doesn't say anything, and he knows he's knocked her out, perhaps given her a concussion. He throws her into the back seat, closes the door, and jumps back behind the wheel. He backs the car up ten feet without even looking and takes off. Later, he will feel lucky that no one else had entered the turn lane after them.

There are four remaining locations for what he wants to do that he has scouted over the past month, and he heads toward the closest one. But first, he pulls in behind a 7-11, next to their trash dumpster, puts the car in park, pops the trunk, jumps out, and grabs the rope and the ball gag. Her body is limp when he ties her up, but she's starting to mumble something when the ball gag goes in her mouth. It takes him a few seconds to buckle the gag behind her head, and then he's back behind the wheel heading south.

24

The shrill ringing of Jeremy Sloan's phone pulled him out of a deep and satisfying slumber. It was still dark. Amanda mumbled next to him and shook his shoulder. Sloan grabbed the phone from the night table and looked at the screen. He didn't recognize the number, but he answered it anyway.

"Sloan," he said, trying not to mumble.

"Hey, it's Donald White. You said to call you if I had another dream."

He sat up. "Yeah." Looking at Amanda still sleeping somewhat fitfully now next to him, he slipped out of bed and walked naked to the kitchen, softly closing Amanda's bedroom door behind him. He could hear crunching, like White was walking on gravel.

"I had another one."

"Are you outside?"

"Yeah. I didn't want to wake Jean."

"All right. What do you remember?"

Sloan turned the kitchen light on and looked in the drawers for something to write with. He finally found a pen in a drawer under the bar. Not seeing any paper, he ripped a paper towel from the roll, set it on the bar, and wrote as White talked.

"He's got a girl in the backseat. That's how they all start. She's tied up and gagged. And he's driving. I remember seeing a Taco Bell on the left when he stops at a red light. He goes again, not driving fast because he doesn't want to get stopped. He's breathing hard, like he always does. There's this heightened sense of awareness whenever I'm in the dream."

"Maybe that's what causes the connection," Sloan said.

"Maybe. Anyway, he's driving, and it seems to take forever. I remember a small marina off to his left and then he's driving over water, a bridge or a causeway or something. Not a big suspension bridge or anything. But a fairly large body of water. After that, he turns left onto what becomes a dirt road. He parks somewhere on that dirt road, picks the girl up out of the backseat, and carries her slung over his shoulder like a sack of potatoes."

"Ok," Sloan said, writing all this down.

It occurred to him that Amanda doesn't live here alone, and he was standing naked in their kitchen. He looked toward her roommate's door, which was open, and thought that the light from the kitchen would surely wake her. He could walk over and shut her door, but a college age girl waking up and finding a naked man in her doorway wouldn't be good optics. So he stood behind the bar to hide himself, ready to tell her to go back to bed should she venture out of her room.

"I don't really want to talk about what he did to her," White said.

"Was it like the others?"

"Yeah. There was a tattoo of a dolphin that he cut off of her. On her right shoulder right around the shoulder blade."

"You didn't see any signs as to where this might be?"

"No. Just the water. So it's by a lake or something."

"OK, I'll look into it."

"Hey," White said before Sloan could end the call.

"Yeah?"

"I've never had dreams like this only a week apart before. What's going on?"

"I wish I knew."

"Sorry to wake you."

"No, you did exactly what I asked you to do. Go back to bed now."

"OK."

Sloan did end the call then. He looked at the phone screen, saw it was 3:55 AM. If he were at home, he could get on his computer and look at a few things. His vehicle outside had a computer in it, but it was usually slow. At home, he could VPN into his workstation at the office and see everything.

Sloan walked back into Amanda's room, shutting off the kitchen light as he went. When he had come over, he hadn't intended on spending the entire night. He could climb back into bed and try to get another two hours of sleep, or he could leave now knowing that he wouldn't be sleeping again for another eighteen or so hours. At this point, he doubted that he'd be able to sleep even if he did lie down and try. So he got dressed in his Friday suit, folding the tie and sticking it in his pocket and just carrying the jacket. He bent down and kissed Amanda.

"I gotta go," he said.

"OK," she mumbled and rolled over.

Sloan stood up straight, took a moment to look at Amanda, and then walked out. Her roommate's bedroom was still open. Now that he was fully clothed, he thought he would close it for her. When he went to grab the door knob, he noticed the bed was empty.

"Hmph," he said and left the door open.

He would have to ask Amanda later if her roommate made a habit out of staying out all night. Rather than boot up the computer in the Navigator, he just drove straight home. It didn't take long with the roads almost deserted at this hour. The first thing he did when he arrived was get out of his suit. One of his tasks later in the day would be to take all his suits to the dry cleaner. He didn't bother getting dressed to sit down at his computer. If the people at that resort did this all the time, he could give it a try. It was more relaxing without the fear of his girlfriend's roommate walking in on him.

He started with a little CYA, covering his own ass. If there had indeed been another homicide overnight, Sloan could just picture either the district attorney or his own supervisor questioning the release of White just a few hours before. He logged in and requested the geo tracking on the phone White had used to call him, which he knew had to be his wife's cell. The image of her rushing out of that trailer without a stitch of clothes on entered his mind, and he had to force it away.

Cell phone geo tracking was a relatively new tool for the FBI although not as new as forensic genetic genealogy which had been used to identify Donald White and then Randall Jacob Crum. Sloan had run the cell phone geo tracking on the sites of the three homicides in Texas, but nothing had shown up. Elena Robles's phone had been left in her car. The other two victim's phones were found in grassy areas near where they had been abducted. But nothing consistent was found at the abduction sites or the sites where the bodies had been found. Sloan therefore had good reason to believe that the suspect didn't carry a cell phone, at least when he was committing his offenses. He was also willing to bet that the guy didn't have a cell phone at all. He was completely off grid.

The geo tracking came back and showed the Whites' phone right where it was supposed to be, just outside of Decatur at the Bluebonnet Nudist Resort. It had moved into Decatur proper for a short time early in the evening, but it had remained at Bluebonnet for the rest of the night.

Sloan then checked last night's police reports and the news sites, but nothing that might be connected to the previous homicides stood out. He checked his email, saw that Captain Mackey had replied to his email about the report on Nancy Janney's murder. From the file, he saw that investigators interviewed three suspects, the ex-husband, the current boyfriend, and her son, Randall Jacob Crum. There hadn't been enough evidence to charge any of them. He skimmed the notes on the interviews with the ex and the boyfriend but gave his full attention to the interview with Crum who claimed to have been on a work trip to New Orleans at the time of the murder. The interviewing officer noted the lack of emotion in Crum's demeanor in spite of the fact that his mother had just been brutally murdered. Sloan then pulled up the psychological profile that had been compiled on the unknown suspect in the cases currently under investigation and read through it again for the twelfth time, making notes about the likelihood of killing his mother. He was still working on it when his cell phone rang.

Pulled out of his computer, Sloan noticed that it was daylight outside as he picked up the phone and saw Amanda's name on the screen.

"Hey Babe," he said.

"Hi. What time was it when you left?"

"Around four."

"Was the door to Marcella's room open when you left?"

"Yeah. I looked in, but she wasn't there."

"I know. She's still not here, and she isn't answering her cell."

"Is it ringing or going straight to voice mail?"

"It's ringing."

Sloan minimized the profile he was editing and the window with his email inbox. The screen for phone geo tracking was still open.

"What's her number?" he asked.

Sloan typed it in as Amanda recited it. He hit the submit button and pulled the profile back up on the screen.

"This isn't like her. She never spends the night out without telling me. And she's always very careful. Not impulsive."

"I'm sure there's a good explanation," Sloan said. "Thank you for last night, by the way."

"That was pretty awesome, wasn't it? We still on for dinner tonight?"

"Absolutely," Sloan replied. "I do have a lot of work before then."

"OK. I'll talk to you later then."

"All right. Bye."

He finished the edits he was making on the profile and pulled up the phone tracking screen. What he saw there made the pit of his stomach fall. Marcella's phone was in the middle of a wooded area alongside Joe Pool Lake. What had White just told him about a large body of water? The spot was at the edge of Tarrant County, so he called one of his contacts in that county's sheriff's department to have someone go check the coordinates given by the phone tracking.

25

The dream last night had been vivid and violent and horrible. Donald had been so exhausted after his jail stint that he had slept through the whole thing. It was only after he had skinned the tattoo off the poor girl's shoulder that he finally woke up, feeling sick and near tears, leaning away from Jean so that he didn't wake her. The notepad and pen on the night table drew his attention. He grabbed them and got up to sit at the dining table which, in the cramped travel trailer, was only three steps away from the bed. Using the moonlight coming in from the window, he tried to remember anything he could about any details of the dream. The only thing that came to mind was the bridge and the water, probably a lake. Donald didn't even bother writing that down.

He crept back into the bedroom, took Jean's phone off the charger, and found the card that Agent Sloan had given them. Donald climbed out of the trailer and stood at the edge of the resort's gravel road to call Sloan. When he finished with the call, he thought about walking up to the hot tub, but he didn't want Jean waking up with him gone, especially when they only had one cell phone between them. When he went back inside the trailer, Jean was awake and in the bathroom.

"You all right?" she asked him.

"I didn't mean to wake you up."

"It's all right. I would have had to pee soon anyway."

She flushed the toilet and climbed back into bed ahead of

Donald. He slipped in after her and plugged her phone back in.

"You had another dream, didn't you?"

"Yeah."

"And you called Agent Sloan."

"Yeah."

"What did he say?"

Donald shrugged. "There wasn't much he could say. But he told me to call him when I had one of those dreams, so I did."

They were silent for a few moments as they both lay in bed looking at the ceiling together.

"You've never had those dreams this close together, have you?" Jean asked.

"No."

"Do you think that's going to look bad? Having a dream the night after you're released?"

"I don't know. I hope not."

After a few more silent minutes, Jean rolled on her side and was asleep again. Donald couldn't say how long he continued to lie awake, but when he did return to sleep, he didn't wake until after nine AM.

Jean was already up, sitting at her laptop at the dining table, typing away.

"Good morning sleepy head," she said when he stood up and staggered to the toilet.

"Hey." After he had peed, he came out and said, "What are you typing?"

"A message to your biological grandmother."

"Oh. Did she write me back?"

"Yes. Come here."

Donald stood over her and looked at the screen. To his last question about how her daughter died, Barbara Janney had written:

Nan was murdered. It still pains me to think about all these years later, but it's not natural, parents burying their children. It should be the children burying the parents. I've just given you access to my private family tree, so if you go there, you can see all the photos I posted of her. A few videos too. I wish you had been able to meet her.

She was your biological mother after all. I feel somewhat guilty that I didn't raise her better than I did, that nothing I did prevented her from following in the path that led to her end. I'm sorry. I can't write anymore right now. Take a look at the photos and let me know what you think.

"Here, sit down," Jean said when she saw that Donald had finished reading.

He sat on the bench beside her, and she started clicking through the photos. They were of a short dark-haired woman with a freckled nose and a crooked smile.

"Oh my God," Donald said when he saw a photo of her sitting on a concrete porch with a six- or seven-year-old boy sitting on the step below her. "He looks just like me. I mean, how I looked at that age."

"I know. I've seen your photos." Jean clicked through a few more until she came to another one with the same woman slightly older and the same boy, now standing beside her and taller than she was.

"This is just weird. It's like I had this whole other life."

"Not you," Jean reminded him.

"But it could have been. That could have been me. And my mother could have wound up with him."

Donald could feel that Jean was about to click the mouse button, so he put his hand over hers. He was still staring at the face of the other son, the face that was identical to his.

"Do you think," he said, his voice cracking just a bit, "if we had been switched, do you think I would have become what he is?"

"No, of course not," Jean answered with no hesitation.

"You're just saying that."

"No, I'm not. I know you. You're not anything like this guy."

"But we started out exactly the same. Identical. Same DNA, same fingerprints, same everything. The only thing that was different between us was our environment. I had my parents, and he had these people. So if I'd been raised by these people, would I have become what he is? And would he have become what I am now?"

"I refuse to believe that. You were you the moment you

were born. And he was what he is."

"But what makes us us? When we start out as newborns, we can't think or reason or make decisions. We eat, sleep, and poop, and we cry when we have issues with any of those things. That's it. We learn to think and to reason and to make decisions based on what's around us. And if things were reversed, I would have learned exactly what this guy learned. I would have become him."

Jean was shaking her head through everything Donald had said. "First of all, we will never ever know what would have happened if the two of you had been switched. For all we know, he still might have become a killer even with your parents raising him."

"That's hard to believe."

"But it could have happened."

Jean took her hand from Donald's and used it to turn his face toward her. "Listen to me Donald White. You are the smartest, kindest man I've ever met. That's who and what you are. And don't ever forget it."

Donald nodded and fought back a tear. "I know. I'm sorry. I just feel like I've had the rug pulled out from under me these past few days, you know. Everything that I've taken for granted as fact throughout my life isn't necessarily so anymore."

"I know. But you have me to lean on. Ok?"

Donald forced a smile at her and kissed her. "Ok."

26

After calling the Tarrant County Sheriff's Department, Jeremy Sloan took a shower, got dressed in his jogging pants, trainers, and FBI t-shirt, and sat back at his computer to wait on the callback. He didn't have to wait long.

"Sloan," he said.

"Your missing person is now a homicide investigation."

"Shit." Sloan was glad he was sitting down because he felt his knees might have just given out.

"I'm sorry. Latina female, approximately five foot three, shoulder length dark hair. Sound like her?"

"Yes. I'm on my way."

He grabbed his keys, badge, and side arm with holster and rushed down to the Navigator. Once he got on the road, his phone rang with Amanda's name popping up on the Lincoln's dash screen. He didn't want to talk to her until he was sure the body found was Marcella, so he let the call go to voicemail. Once it did, he hit the button to call Sam Blackman.

"Hello," Sam answered after the first ring.

"Sam, we got another homicide out at Joe Pool Lake."

"Jesus. It's only been a week. Do you really think it's our guy?"

"I have reason to believe it is."

"All right. It'll take me a bit to get there."

"No problem."

The entrance to the section of the park where the body had

been found was already marked off with a sheriff's deputy parked at the turn off. He took a look at Sloan's ID and moved his vehicle long enough for Sloan to get through. He parked the Navigator behind six other police vehicles and a crime scene van, and followed the narrow walking trail to the site. The body was still there, with photographers marking things and snapping photos. Plaster molds were being taken of the footprints up to the scene. All Sloan needed was to see the body's face, and when he did, he had to work hard to maintain his normal stoic expression. It was Marcella, but she was far different from the happily curious young woman he had just spoken to the night before. She was nude, lying on her back, her arms and legs spread out in what looked like a cross. Her throat had been sliced open and her mouth was frozen in a heartbreaking expression of pained bewilderment.

Lieutenant Mark Starr, the man he had called earlier that morning after the geo tracking had displayed her phone's location, was there and had taken charge of the scene.

"Did you know her?" he asked.

"Barely," Sloan answered, trying to minimize his personal involvement.

"This couldn't be your guy, could it? I thought he was already in custody."

"We've had a highly unusual set of circumstances regarding that. Which is all going to have to be made public now."

"So you think it is your guy?"

"Yeah."

"Well shit."

"Tell me about it."

Sloan wandered around the edge of the scene, staying out of the lab techs' way, but he had seen all he needed to see. The suspect had been identified; now he just needed to be captured. Sloan had to put his personal disgust and sadness aside and think about the situation. There were over seven and a half million people in the Dallas-Fort Worth metroplex, approximately 3.75 million of whom were women. Marcella did fit the demographic of Crum's other victims, but his just happening to find and kill Marcella out of all of those 3.75 million women was much too large of a coincidence for Sloan to believe. No, Crum knew who Sloan was and knew where his girlfriend lived. This was no coincidence; this was a message.

"Fuck," Sloan said.

He rushed back to the Navigator and took off back toward Arlington with the flashing blue and red lights in the grill turned on, slowing down only to let the deputy guarding the entrance to the scene move out of his way. He turned on his siren when he had to get through intersections and arrived at Amanda's apartment in less than half an hour. Pulling his Glock from the holster, he made sure the first round was chambered and headed to Amanda's door with it held in front of him in a ready position.

He tried to open the door and found it locked. *Good job Amanda*, he thought. He then knocked on the door and listened. Footsteps approached the door.

"Who is it?" Amanda asked.

"It's Jeremy."

Sloan could see the peephole darken, glad to see that she had checked. The lock clicked, and the door opened. Sloan rushed inside past Amanda and ran through each room of the apartment.

"Has anybody been here?" he asked.

"No. What is the matter with you?"

"Nothing. Pack a bag. You can't stay here."

"I live here."

Sloan began to relax, seeing for himself that the apartment was empty besides Amanda, but he soon realized he didn't have anywhere to safely stow his gun as he had left the holster in the car.

"I know, but you're at risk here."

"Jeremy, what's the matter? Did you find out anything about Marcella?"

He shook his head meekly, needing to tell her but not wanting to. Setting the gun on the bar between the living room and kitchen, he turned and took Amanda by the shoulders, started to say it but choked up.

"Marcella!" Amanda gasped.

Sloan was still shaking his head. "I'm sorry. But we have to get you out of here."

"Why? Why Marcella?" Amanda was crying now, wringing

her hands as she walked around the apartment.

"Amanda, we need to go. Now."

Sloan picked up the Glock from the bar as Amanda threw an overnight bag together. He kept his head on a swivel as they walked out of the apartment, trying to watch from all directions and pausing only so Amanda could lock the front door. Once they were in the car, Sloan holstered his weapon and drove toward his apartment.

"Marcella fit the demographic of this guy's past victims," Sloan told the sobbing Amanda. "He must have followed me to your place. That won't happen again."

Sloan could only assume that Crum didn't know where he lived, so he performed four U-turns on his unconventional route home to make sure no one was following them. Sam called while they were en route.

"Hey, where did you go?" Sam said.

"I had to pick up my girlfriend. That's her roommate out at Joe Pool Lake."

"Holy shit!"

"Yeah."

"They're going to take you off this case. You know that don't you."

"I know. Not if I can catch the guy first though."

"How are you going to do that?"

"He had to have followed me last night. As soon as I get home, I'm pulling up the traffic cameras from last night's commute. If we can lock onto a vehicle, we can lock onto him."

"Good idea."

"Stick with the coroner. Let me know their preliminary findings."

"Will do."

They were almost to Sloan's apartment when Amanda said, "He followed you to my place?"

"That's the only explanation."

"My God. Marcella died because I wanted to date an FBI agent."

"It's not your fault."

"Yeah, it kind of is."

Sloan didn't know what to say to this, so he kept quiet. When they got to his place, he ushered Amanda inside, carrying the holster but leaving the Glock in it.

"I have some work to do," he said. "There's drinks in the fridge and snacks in the kitchen if you want anything."

Sloan logged back into his computer and pulled up three traffic camera feeds. He found his Lincoln on the first one, froze the image, and went to the second camera about a mile away. He found his Lincoln there and froze that image. There, two cars back in the first shot and four cars back in the second was a dark blue Toyota Corolla, at least twenty years old. He pulled the plate number off it and ran it against the state database. It was a 2001 Corolla registered to Walter Mott who lived at 2200 Aden Road, Apartment 607. The registration was only two months old. Just for redundancy, Sloan found his Navigator on the third traffic camera and spotted that same Corolla in that shot too, three cars behind his. He pulled up the driver's license for the Walter Mott on Aden Road and saw Randall Jacob Crum's unsmiling face staring back at him.

His next call was to assistant DA Lawrence DeLuca so he could get an arrest and search warrant issued. He then put out an APB on that 2001 Corolla just in case it happened to be involved in a traffic stop in the next couple of hours. Changing out of his workout clothes and into a proper suit, he headed out the door.

"Amanda, honey, I have to go to work for a bit. You'll be all right here. Keep the door locked and don't let anyone in, all right."

"OK." She was sitting on the living room sofa staring at the TV that wasn't powered on.

"You need anything, call me, OK?"

"OK," she said again, almost in a trance.

Sloan paused at the door, looking at her. "I'm sorry," he said again and left, locking the door behind him.

27

Between FBI personnel, Tarrant County Sheriff's deputies, and Fort Worth Police Department officers, the Aden Crest apartment complex was invaded that Saturday. The apartment complex manager, a middle-aged woman with squinty eyes and a facial tic, had given Sloan a key to apartment 607 after he told her they would break the door in if they didn't have a way to unlock it. The apartment itself was on the second floor with the entrance facing the parking lot, the back door and balcony overlooking Aden Road.

Once Sloan had the key and was walking from the office to Crum's apartment, he gave the signal for everyone else to converge. He bounded up the stairs as the parking lot filled with cop cars. Agent Blackman was right behind him followed by two police sergeants and two deputies. They all crowded onto the landing, guns drawn. Once they got the radio signal that everyone was in position to prevent any escape out the back balcony, Sloan slid the key into the lock and turned it as quietly as he could. Once it was unlocked, he banged the door open, announcing, "POLICE!"

But there was nothing more to say. The apartment was empty. There was no furniture, no people, no nothing. In fact, it looked ready to show to prospective tenants. The single bedroom and bathroom along with the closets were all just as clean and empty as the rest of the apartment.

"Well, shit," Sam said.

"He's probably moved to a whole new alias," Sloan said.

"Yeah."

Sloan stalked back to the apartment manager's office.

"Apartment 607 has been cleaned out," he told her.

"Oh my."

"How did he normally pay his rent?"

She stood and opened a drawer in the filing cabinet behind her. "We don't take cash," she said as she pulled a folder from the drawer. She placed it on the desk in front of Sloan.

He opened it up and saw a photocopy of a United States Postal Service money order, dated June 30th. There were three other copies just like it in the file, each dated the last day of the previous months.

"He's been here four months?" Sloan asked.

"Three. One of those is his deposit."

"Did he sign a lease?" Sloan said just as he uncovered a copy of the lease agreement.

"Yes, six months."

"Did he leave any kind of notice that he was moving out?"

"No."

"When was the last time you saw him?"

"I don't remember. I think I saw him walking past the office four days ago."

Sloan pulled up Donald White's mugshot on his phone. "Just for the record, this is the person we're talking about, right?"

The apartment manager squinted at the phone screen and slowly nodded. "Yes, that looks like him. But that's the photo I saw on the news yesterday."

"That's right. But it could be a picture of the man you know as Walter Mott, right?"

"Oh yeah. I remember saying to Harold — that's my husband — Harold, when we were watching the news last night, I said, that looks just like the tenant in 607. So Harold says, 'Maybe it *is* him.' And I said, 'Maybe it is.' It is, isn't it? You already have him in jail."

"I can't divulge too much in an active investigation."

"Sure. Sure."

Sloan got away from the apartment office as quickly as he could while still being diplomatic. Once outside, he called

Assistant DA DeLuca.

"So this is a nightmare, isn't it," DeLuca said after the greetings were made.

"What's that?"

"We release a suspect, and another murder happens that very night."

"No one knew we had let him out," Sloan said.

"What's that supposed to mean?"

"It means the perpetrator didn't know we had let him out."

"The perpetrator? So you still don't think this Donald White is the perpetrator?"

"Of course he's not. I know right where he was all night, and it wasn't anywhere near Joe Pool Lake."

"So what do you need?"

"A press conference. Clearing White and alerting the public to Randal Jacob Crum aka Walter Mott."

"You mean, go public with the whole twins story?"

"Yes."

"That's crazy."

"It will get people talking. Everyone will be looking for him at that point. He won't be able to go anywhere under whatever new alias he has. Besides, you need to talk about the new murder."

"And you're sure this new one is the same guy?"

"Yeah. It won't take long for DNA to confirm it anyway, but yeah, I'm sure."

"All right. I'll call a press conference for this afternoon."

"Good."

"How close are you to catching him?"

"We're breathing down his neck." He didn't want to tell him that they had no clue what alias he was now using or where he had gone.

"Good. I'll type up a speech and send it to you."

"I'll be looking for it."

Sloan ended the call and stalked back to the Lincoln. Sam was waiting there for him.

"What now?"

Sloan shook his head. "I don't know. It would be nice to get ahead of this guy for once."

"He sure is a bold bastard. Following you like he did."

"Yeah. Why would he do that?"

"Maybe he's jealous."

"Jealous how?"

"You arrested someone else for his crimes. Maybe he didn't like anyone else taking credit for what he did."

"Interesting. I was thinking he killed another victim so we would realize we had the wrong guy. Remember, he doesn't know we already let White out of jail."

"Yeah. You think he plans these things or acts on impulse?"

"He has to plan them. If he didn't, someone would have caught him long before now."

"Yeah."

Sloan opened his car door and slid behind the wheel. "I'm going to head home for awhile. I've got a grieving and scared girlfriend there."

"Good luck with that."

On his way home, he called Jean White's phone. Donald answered right away.

"Hello."

"Mr. White, this is Special Agent Sloan. How are you today?"

"I'm all right. A little bored."

"Well, there have been some developments in the case."

"Was there another killing?"

"Sadly, yes."

"Dammit."

"We are announcing your release today, so you can go home whenever you feel like it."

"Wonderful. Do you know how difficult it is to stay in this trailer when I can hear all the activity up at the pool?

"I can only imagine. What time do you think you'll be home?"

"We're probably going to leave in the next hour."

"How about I stop by today around six PM? I have some things to give you. Cell phone, computer."

"That'll be awesome. We'll be there then."

"All right. See you at six."

Sloan hung up, feeling a bit unsure about what he planned on talking to them about when he did visit their house. But at the moment, it was the best shot he had.

28

Jean was more than happy that Donald wanted to go straight home rather than spend the rest of the weekend at the resort. The last few days had taken it out of them both. Jean was also sure that Donald missed his own bed. The trailer bed was OK for a getaway but was a poor substitute for home. He dressed in the only clothes he had, the khaki pants and polo shirt he had worn to work on Thursday, which seemed like a lifetime ago. It seemed strange to see him so well dressed at the resort where the standard dress for arriving or departing was shorts and t-shirt with nudity in between.

"I'm sorry the house is a mess," she had told him when they walked in. "The FBI didn't clean up after themselves."

Donald shrugged and made his way to their bedroom. He had told her that Agent Sloan was stopping by at six, so both of them stayed dressed, with Donald changing out of the three-day-old work clothes and into a pair of denim shorts and a Texas Rangers t-shirt.

"You hungry?" he asked after plopping himself down on the love seat next to her.

"Starved," she said. She'd actually started to suggest stopping for dinner on the way home, but she knew how anxious Donald was to get home after his nights in jail and the trailer.

They ordered sandwiches from a nearby deli using Uber Eats and ate them in the living room with the season four finale of *Stranger Things* on the TV. They had finished eating but hadn't finished the show when the doorbell rang. Donald paused the episode and got up to answer, peeking through the peephole first.

"It's him," he said to Jean before opening the door.

"Hello. Is this a good time?" she heard the agent ask as she stood up and walked to the door.

"Yeah, it's fine."

Donald let Agent Sloan inside. He was carrying a box, and in that box, she could see their computer with evidence stickers still on the PC.

"I've got another box out in the car," he said.

"Thanks." Donald took the first one from him and walked into the dining room with it.

"Would you like anything to drink?" Jean asked when Agent Sloan had returned with the second box.

"No, I'm good. Thanks."

Donald took the second box, which contained items from their freezer among other things. Agent Sloan sat on the sofa where Jean had motioned. He looked at the small marble sculpture on the end table next to him.

"That's Athena," Jean told him. "My grandmother carved it."

Agent Sloan picked it up as if weighing it in his hand. "It's good," he said.

"Thank you."

He set it back down on the end table.

Donald walked back into the living room with his phone in his hand. He plugged it into the charging cable on the end table next to the love seat and sat down.

"So how is everything going with the case?" Donald asked.

"Well, we identified Crum's alias and the car he's been using, but he appears to have moved on."

"Damn."

"The car did turn up in the parking lot of Weatherford College this afternoon, so they think he's moving back west."

"'They' think that." Jean said. "But you don't?"

"No, I don't."

"Why not?"

"Because he's making it too obvious. Why park the car at a

college where it will quickly draw a citation? Why not park it at a Walmart instead where it could sit for days before being found?"

"You're the only one who realizes this?" Donald asked.

"No. But a lot of agencies are anxious to be rid of him. They see what they want to see when it appears that he's left the area."

"So where do you think he's going?"

Sloan shifted in his seat and took a deep breath. "I think he's coming here."

"Here?" Jean said. "As in our house?"

"He's a narcissistic sociopath. I don't think he can resist seeing someone who is basically a carbon copy of himself. So yes, I think he'll try to come here. To your house."

Jean and Donald looked at each other.

"It is just a hunch though," Sloan added.

"So what do we do?" Donald asked.

"We can do it one of two ways. You can avoid him by moving into a safe house until we catch him. Or you can stay here under observation and help us catch him when he comes."

"Run and hide or become bait in a trap. I don't like either one of those options." Donald looked at Jean as he said it.

She shrugged.

"We'll catch him a lot faster, I think, if you stay here. If we do that, I will plant a few listening devices around your house, and someone nearby would be listening at all times."

"Just listening devices?" Jean asked.

"Yes. Why?"

"We, well…" She looked at Donald who nodded to her. "We tend to be practicing nudists when we're at home. Unless we are expecting company. Like now. Ha."

Agent Sloan kept a straight face and said, "No cameras. Audio only."

"Thank you."

"Do you think we're in real danger?" Donald asked.

"Anybody who deals with Randall Jacob Crum is in danger. In your case though, being identical to him in almost every way, I have no idea how he will react. And I may be wrong. He may not come anywhere near here. But something tells me that his own curiosity will get the better of him."

"You're going to have people both watching the house and listening?"

"Yes."

"For how long?" Jean asked.

Sloan shifted in his seat. "Well, we don't have the manpower to do it indefinitely. I'm betting that if he does come here, it will be soon. Like within a couple of days."

"So does that mean you'll only have someone watching the house for a couple of days then?" Donald asked.

"Like I said, this is just a hunch. I hope he doesn't show up here. I hope he leaves you both alone and that we catch him somewhere else very very soon. But I can't ignore what my gut is telling me. I'll have someone watching the house for as long as I can. But I also think that if he doesn't show here within three or four days, then he's not going to. He's on the run, and he knows it. He'll probably try to find a place to hide for a long time."

Jean looked at Donald who kept his attention on Agent Sloan. He finally nodded and said, "OK."

"Good," Sloan said. "I'll go ahead and plant the microphones around the house, one here in the living room, one in the kitchen, and one in your master bedroom, if that's all right."

"Sure," Donald said.

"And I'll need your Wi-Fi password so I can listen even away from the house."

Donald spelled out the password as Sloan typed it into an app on his phone. Jean then watched him take three white devices out of his pocket, unplug the lamp in the living room, plug one of those devices into the wall socket, and replug the lamp cord in over that. He then disappeared into the kitchen with Donald following him to see where the devices were placed.

"Now, start talking to each other," Sloan said when he and Donald walked back into the living room.

"I don't know what to say," Jean said.

"Testing, one, two, three, I guess," Donald added.

Sloan had been standing looking at his phone with one hand and the other over one of his ears. He nodded and gave them a thumbs up. "Good," he said. "Now, if he does wind up getting past us and into the house, just say Volkswagen. You can work it into conversation even. If you say that, we'll come running." He paused a moment, looking at Jean and Donald. "We need a quick way into the house."

"Hold on," Donald said. He disappeared into the kitchen and came back with their spare key. "This will work on the front door."

"Thanks, that's great," Sloan said, taking it and slipping it into his pocket. He looked at both of them again. "I guess that's it then."

"Thank you," Donald said, "for everything."

"Don't thank me yet. We don't know what's going to happen. Stay safe."

29

He is used to feelings of paranoia. But is it really paranoia when everyone really is out to get you? His face is all over the TV news, the Internet, and the newspapers, if anyone still reads those. This might have made switching personas and vehicles somewhat tricky, but there are still enough people wearing masks after Covid that he could wear one without drawing much attention to himself. He then played musical vehicles, driving the eighteen-year-old Nissan Maxima he had bought from a we-tote-the-note place in Saginaw two months ago into Weatherford, parking it in an Albertson's parking lot not far from the college, hot-wiring and stealing another car from that college, driving the stolen car back to Fort Worth and abandoning it in at the mall by his old apartment, and then driving the Walter Mott-registered Corolla back to Weatherford, parking it at the college, and walking to the Albertson's to get the Maxima. The riskiest part of all that was having to leave his belongings, especially the trophies, in the Maxima while it was parked in Weatherford. But everything turned out all right.

Now, he has a clean, state issued ID under the name of Edward Ganske (even if it's not a full driver's license) and a car purchased and legally registered under that name. His only problem now is his face. During the day, he hides behind a Texas Rangers baseball cap, a large pair of sunglasses, and one of those surgical masks. At night, the sunglasses are too conspicuous, so he has been staying in the motel room he has rented for the week. This time of year, the nights are short, thankfully. Tonight though, he has to go out. But when he leaves the relative safety of the car, no one will see him.

He parks five blocks away from the guy's house and walks in the shadows to the street behind the guy's backyard. He remembers the street number, and when he sees that same number on the parallel street, he crosses, slips between two houses and stops at the gate of a six foot wooden privacy fence, listening for any dogs. He tries the gate, letting the latch rattle just enough to rouse any dogs. There are none, and the gate is unlocked, which saves him the trouble of scaling the fence and jumping to the ground on the other side.

He peeks around the corner of the house to make sure the residents aren't out in the backyard at two in the morning for some reason. No one is there, and the patio lights are off, although a bit of dim light is coming from the windows. He sprints to the back corner and uses that corner to lift himself up and over the fence, allowing himself to fall into the back corner of the next yard. The gun in his pocket feels heavy as it slaps against his leg when he hits the ground. It is a compact Ruger .38, taken from the car of one of his girls a few years ago. He has never shot it, so he isn't even sure it will fire. But people will do things at gun point that they won't do at knifepoint. Not that he has a plan for that. Not yet anyway.

He is now in *his* back yard, the man with his face. The rear of the house is dark. He slinks up to the back door and stops to listen, his ear against the glass. The kitchen is on the other side of the door, he remembers from his last visit. He tries the doorknob just in case they forgot to lock it, but locked it is.

His lock picking kit is in his hip pocket, and it takes him less than two minutes to get the door unlocked. When he hears the click, he packs up his kit and takes a moment to gather himself before he opens the door. When he looks inside, he sees the digital readout on the microwave over the range displays the time, 2:13. He steps inside and eases the door closed, locking it back and wincing at the soft click that it makes. The house is quiet. He stands beside the back door listening for any indication of movement. There is none. He creeps through the kitchen and dining room and turns into the hall. The sound of snoring reaches him, and he stops and looks into the master bedroom, watching the two of them sleep.

What am I doing here? He asks himself this question, and he can't give a good answer. He's curious about this guy with his face and his life. His mother, the bitch, sent him away when he was a baby, depriving him of a brother and a playmate. Why did she send this guy away and keep him? Why couldn't it have been the other way around? If it had, would it be him sleeping in that bed with the woman? And would it be the other guy who had this obsession, this urge that he couldn't fight and couldn't live without? He is here, he supposes, because he wants at least a taste of this guy's life. And if it leads to the end of everything, will it be worth it? He doesn't know and supposes that he won't know until it happens, *if* it happens.

When the man shifts in his sleep, turning from his left to his right side, he slinks away, slipping into the guest room. The bed is still there, still made up just as it was the last time he was here. Dropping to his knees, he lies down and scoots under the bed, taking care to arrange the fabric of the bed skirt back the way it had been. He will stay here and wait. For what, he doesn't know. He could go to sleep, but he doesn't want to snore himself and alert the man or his wife. So he keeps waking himself every time he begins to drift off.

30

After the argument with Amanda at his apartment Saturday, Jeremy Sloan decided to take the Sunday night graveyard shift surveilling Donald and Jean White's house himself. He had spent the previous night there after having planted the listening devices Saturday evening, leaving at six AM Sunday when Sam Blackman relieved him. Sloan had been so preoccupied with the case, trying to find Crum before his likely removal from the case on Monday, that he had forgotten that Amanda had been stuck at his apartment until he got home.

"I'm sorry," he said when he walked in and found her lying on his couch, half asleep.

She sighed and said, "When can I go back to my apartment?"

"Soon, I hope. First thing I have to do is get a few hours of sleep."

Sloan left her on the couch, peeled his clothes off, and got into bed. As tired as he was, he still had trouble turning his brain off. He had been on his way home from Crum's apartment when he got the call that the car had been found in the parking lot of Weatherford College. After an immediate U-turn, he was there in less than half an hour. The crime scene unit there in Parker County collected any and all hair and stain samples from inside the car, and the results of testing such materials was still pending. Nothing beyond such trace evidence had been left in the car, and there wasn't much else to do there in Weatherford, so he had gone back to the office to collect the belongings for the Whites and meet them at their house. He had then walked their neighborhood before settling in for a long night of surveillance.

He had, of course, remembered to call Amanda and cancel their planned Saturday evening dinner date. He could tell that she had been angry but had been holding it in, sounding like she was gritting her teeth when she spoke. He had expected her to blow up at him. But instead of blowing a fuse, she sounded very calm as she acknowledged his absence. That calmness concerned him more than an angry outburst would have. And she had still seemed calm when he had come in and gone to bed.

But he had to stop thinking about Amanda and concentrate on Crum. Sloan had been two steps behind ever since Crum had been identified as the suspect, and his stake out of the Whites' house was his Hail Mary attempt to get ahead of him. But what was he going to do if Crum didn't show up this weekend? Because one of the victims now had a personal connection to him, he knew the case was going to go to someone else. What would Sloan do then, leave the Whites out to dry or keep up with the surveillance? And if he kept up with the surveillance, how long could he keep it up? Would they allocate man-hours to it, or would he have to shoulder the whole thing?

The questions kept swirling in his head, but they must have stopped long enough to allow him to sleep because the next thing he knew, Amanda was shaking his shoulder.

"Hey," she had said.

Sloan bolted upright, looking at Amanda and the room. "What?" he said when he realized there was no emergency.

"I just got an Uber. He's going to take me home."

It took a second for that to register.

"No. I don't want you at your apartment."

"I'm not going to stay there. I'm going to get a few things and drive to my dad's house."

Sloan shook his head, trying to emerge from the sleep fog and focus. "I'd rather you stay here."

"Why? So I can sit alone and watch your TV. It's not like you're here to protect me."

"I'm trying to catch this guy."

"Well, you can do that whether I'm here or at my dad's. I shouldn't be here anyway."

"What's that supposed to mean?" Sloan asked, slipping out of bed as Amanda left the room.

He followed her into the living room.

"It means that I shouldn't be here. As in we shouldn't be together. Marcella died because I've been dating you."

"No. She died because of a sociopathic killer."

"Who would never have crossed paths with her if it wasn't for *you*." The emphasis on that last word turned the entire statement into an accusation. Her phone dinged, and she looked at the screen. "My ride's here."

"I'm sorry Amanda. I didn't mean for any of that to happen."

She opened the door and looked back at him. "I'm sorry too. And I'm sorry I could never compete with your job. Your precious Bureau."

Amanda slammed the door shut behind her.

"Fuck," Sloan said and started to walk out after her before realizing he was naked and his apartment was not in the resort where the Whites went every weekend.

He could have guessed that he and Amanda would have problems after what had happened to her roommate, but his sole focus over the past two days had been finding the bastard who had killed Marcella. Once Crum was behind bars, Sloan figured that he and Amanda could then work on patching up their relationship. But now, it appeared there would be no relationship to patch up. Still, Sloan created a small gap in the window blinds and watched to make sure Amanda got in the car without any issues. The car was a late model white Prius, and the driver appeared to be a black male who in no way looked like Randall Jacob Crum. Once the Prius disappeared from sight, Sloan released the blinds and went back to bed.

His phone display told him that it was already five PM. He tried to sleep another hour or two, but his brain was fully active again. After thirty minutes of lying on the bed, he gave up and rolled into his bathroom. The hot shower helped lessen that feeling of fatigue.

On his way to the Whites' house to relieve Sam, his phone

rang.

"Sloan," he said.

"Agent Sloan, this is Donald White."

"Hi Mr. White, how are you? Is everything all right?"

"Oh yeah, everything is fine. I just wanted to tell you that Jean and I both need to go into work tomorrow. So the house will be empty most of the day."

"That's all right."

"I don't know if you want to keep watching it or follow us to work or what?"

"You leave that to us. OK?"

"All right."

"For now, I'll be outside your house all night tonight. I'll have to leave and head to the office about the same time you and Jean are leaving."

"You're going to work after not sleeping all night?"

"I've done it before."

He didn't tell them that he dreaded what might happen at the office on Monday.

Now, as he sat in the Navigator three houses down from the Whites' house at three AM on a Monday morning in July, running the motor every once in a while to keep the interior cool and watching for any moving shadows on the street or in the yards, he considered, maybe for the first time since training at Quantico, leaving the Bureau. He was good at his job, but it had already cost him a lot in his personal life already. Hell, he didn't even have a personal life anymore. He lived, breathed, and slept FBI work. It was beginning to be too much. And when the inevitable happens, when he goes into the office in the morning and is removed as the lead investigator on the Crum murders, how will he react, especially given his lack of sleep and the loss of Amanda? At the moment, he couldn't say. If he wasn't afraid of falling asleep, he would close his eyes and do some deep breathing techniques.

The sky gradually lightened, and nothing more interesting than an occasional car passing by happened on the Whites' street. He watched Donald and Jean walk outside together, share a kiss between their two vehicles, and drive away in different directions. He was about to head home for a quick shower and shave before going to the office when he heard noises on the phone app, clicking and tapping from inside the Whites' house. Sloan cut the engine of the Navigator, got out with his Glock in hand, and started creeping toward the house, cutting through yards instead of keeping to the sidewalk. Once he got in front of the Whites' house, he crawled just under the front bay windows until he got to their front porch. Taking the key out of his pocket, he inserted it into the lock and turned it slowly. Once he heard the click, he pushed the door open and burst into the living room, Glock in the ready position.

All was quiet. The ceiling fan in the living room was turning, but there was otherwise no movement. Sloan stood up straight, turned back toward the door, took the key out of the lock, and closed it. He turned and walked slowly through the house, looking and listening. The living room was neat, but the master bedroom was a mess, the bed unmade, dirty clothes piled on the floor in the corner.

"Hello, this is Agent Sloan of the Federal Bureau of Investigation," he called, but there was no answer.

The central air conditioner, which had been quiet up until then, kicked back on. Sloan wondered if the slight rattle of it revving back up was what he had heard before. He looked into the closets and the bathrooms, just to make sure, but there appeared to be no one in the house. Still, something didn't feel right. But he didn't have time to reflect on it. He had to get to the office.

<h1 style="text-align:center">31</h1>

He lies under the bed on his side, listening to the man and the woman talk in the morning. He hears the shower in the master bedroom turn on for about six minutes, then off for about three, and then on for almost ten.

"I'm not looking forward to the questions," he hears the man say from the hall a bit later.

"Me either," the woman replies. "But we have to get it over with sooner or later. I'd rather it be sooner, so we can move on."

They continue talking as they walk out the door. He hears the lock click, but he waits a bit before scooting out from under the guest bed. After taking a moment to stretch the sore muscles, he walks to the master bedroom. The first thing he notices is that the bed is unmade. There is a pile of dirty clothes in the corner. He walks in and looks in the closet, seeing the man's clothes. He pulls a pair of khakis from a hanger and lays it on the bed, goes back to the closet and finds a blue Polo shirt and lays it on the bed on top of the khakis. He then strips out of his black shirt and pants and throws them onto the pile of clothes in the corner. His lock picking kit and the Ruger he lays on the bed next to the clothes.

He puts the Polo shirt on and has the khakis in his hand when he hears the front door burst open. His first thought was that if they have a bunch of stuff under their bed, he will have to use the Ruger, but he grabs it and the kit and, with the pants still in his hand, drops to the floor and rolls under the bed. There are a few boxes, but there is room for him to fit and remain hidden behind the sheets that are hanging down almost to the floor. He is on the side of the bed away from the door, so that should give him some protection. Footsteps approach the master bedroom. He thinks of the old saying, "caught with your pants down" and has to stifle a laugh as he doesn't even have pants on.

"Hello, this is Agent Sloan of the Federal Bureau of Investigation."

He feels a surge of fear and self-loathing. He knows his taking of the girl from the apartment Sloan went to will make Sloan vengeful. If he really wanted to end things, he could roll out from under the bed with the gun in his hand and let Sloan shoot him dead. But he doesn't do that. He wants to see the man who lives here, the man with his face.

Agent Sloan walks into the bedroom, looks in the closet and the bathroom, only his feet visible. He holds the Ruger pointed out, ready to pull the trigger if Sloan looks under the bed. The FBI agent doesn't, and he hears him walk back out of the room.

He waits until he hears the front door open and close, and the lock click, and then he waits some more. When he's finally sure Sloan is gone, he rolls out from under the bed and walks around the house with the Ruger in his hand. He wishes again that he had fired the Ruger at least once so he will know it will work. But he can't test it here, now, so he can only hope he doesn't have to fire it later today, whatever happens.

That gets him wondering just what he thought he was going to accomplish by coming here. If he had any sense, he would be heading somewhere far away. But part of him also says, *why bother?* Thanks to the DNA thing and his identical twin, police everywhere know exactly what he looks like. His photo or this Donald White's photo, it didn't matter. They might as well be of the same person. He supposes that he could alter his appearance, grow a beard or alter his face some other way, put a big scar down his cheek. But such a scar would draw more attention than he ever wants. And no matter what he did, he could never change his DNA signature.

The idea that came to him the previous night is to kill the woman and the man and take over the man's identity. They'd think the woman's husband had killed him for killing his wife. The only problem with that was, he'd still have to leave. He couldn't do the man's job. He didn't even know what the man's job was, much less any of the people there. No, he'd have to pretend to be so traumatized by what had happened that he'd have to leave the state. And then the police would still be watching him, tracking him, just to make sure. Not that he could ever voluntarily give up adding to his girls. His heart begins to beat faster just thinking of the one the other night. How could that ever end?

He thinks of Peggy now. Peggy Kirkwood. He supposes that he thinks about her at some point each and every day. She was his first. The first girl he kissed. The first girl he fucked. The first girl he possessed. The first kiss had been exciting. Until then, no one had taken much of an interest in him. A few months later, he sneaked her into his bedroom where they fooled around. He had fucked her, but he could never finish, not that she ever noticed. He wondered if he hadn't masturbated so much that he was unable to ejaculate with a woman like he was supposed to. He still couldn't come the next two times they did it, and he had to wonder what all the fuss from the other guys at school was about. It didn't seem that great to him. But Peggy wanted to keep meeting up. She was never that bright. The fourth time, he put his hands around her throat as they fucked. He saw her excitement turn to fear as he kept squeezing and fucking. She fought back, tried to push him away, but he kept his hold on her and kept thrusting into her again and again. When he came, it was like nothing he'd ever felt before, an explosion. When he let go of Peggy's neck, she didn't move. Her eyes, which had just a few moments before bulged out of their sockets, stared back at him, but there was nothing behind the eyes. Peggy was dead.

He was torn about it. The experience of it had been extraordinary, but Peggy was no longer there to fool around with. He also had the problem of what to do with the body. Luckily, Peggy had been a petite girl, and he could carry her a long way if needed. Being still in high school at the time, he had no car, so he carried her into the woods behind the abandoned shack where they had been meeting for sex. He took her to a spot he knew well. When he was younger, he had brought stray cats and dogs there and experimented on them. He left her between two big tree roots, covering her with leaves and dirt. When he got back with a pick and a shovel, an animal had chewed part of her hand off. Two of her fingers were missing. He scoured the area around the two roots. Three buzzards were flying overhead, and he remembers wondering if one of them might have flown off with the fingers. That prompted him to give up the search.

He dug a hole away from the tree roots as deep as he could get it, which was only about four feet or so, and buried Peggy in it. When the police came around two days later asking questions, he thought they would see through his lies. He and Peggy were both loners in school, so it was easy to claim that he didn't know her that well since there wasn't anyone else to rebut him. When they left, he lived for several days in expectation of being arrested at any minute. But they never came back. Of course, Peggy was always listed a missing person. As far as he knows, they never found her body or her missing fingers.

As the days passed, his fear of being found out lessened. It also became easier for him to do whatever he wanted as time marched on. Once he'd crossed the line and done something that would get him executed, he felt an enormous freedom to do anything. That all boiled over when his bitch mother pissed him off for the last time. Unlike Peggy, they found her body, but he wasn't worried about it. He'd left enough at the scene that the police would suspect her latest boyfriend, although they never arrested that asshole. They had even talked to him about the murder, but he claimed ignorance of any facts. Still, the fear was there, but it, once again, lessened as time marched on.

That rush he felt when he'd killed Peggy drew him to more girls, and he found that it was easier to be on the road than to stay in one place. He'd also realized that he needed other names, so he'd acquired the birth certificates of four boys who would have been close to the same age as he was had they not died very young. This was back when birth certificates had been easier to get. The last time he'd tried to get someone's birth certificate, they had wanted proof that he was some kind of relative or that he had a legitimate need to acquire that certificate. He'd walked out of the county office empty handed and swore he'd never go back. But with the original four birth certificates he'd obtained, it was easy to get ID's under those names. Edward Ganske is the last of those, but it hardly matters now. With his face everywhere in the media, it's only a matter of time before he's found. But then he had known for a long time that he'd be found eventually.

He wanders back to the master bedroom and puts the man's pants on. He wears his own socks, and he doesn't need shoes in the house. The little Ruger goes into his front pants pocket. He leaves his lock picking kit on the dresser. He probably won't ever need it again after today. There is a knife block in the kitchen, and he takes the chef's knife out and carries it into the living room. He sits on the couch in silence, waiting and wondering what it was like to live in a house like this.

32

Despite leaving the house early, Jean didn't get to work until five after eight. By the time she got to her desk, she had already fielded four questions about how she was coping with her husband's arrest and release and the fact that he was an identical twin to a serial murderer.

"For right now, I'm just glad he's home," she had answered to all four of the people who questioned her. "We're still figuring everything else out."

She'd been at her desk for only fifteen minutes before Brandon, her manager, sent her an instant message asking her to come into his office. Wondering how she was supposed to get any work done with everyone fawning over her, she got up and trudged over to Brandon's corner office.

"Jean," he said when she entered. "Close the door."

"What's up Brandon?" she said after she had closed it.

"I really didn't expect to see you for a while."

Jean shrugged. "Here I am."

"Are you sure you're ready to jump back in?"

"I was only out one day."

"I know. But I've seen the news. I know the turmoil you're going through."

"The turmoil is over. Donald has been cleared and is home. So I'm here."

Brandon sighed and leaned back in his chair. "You know the Asymetrix project is on a tight timeline."

"Yeah, and we've been running ahead of schedule."

"I reassigned it to Barb."

"You did what?"

"Jean, I had every expectation that you would be out a week or more, hiring attorneys, building a defense, visiting your husband, that sort of thing."

"Thank God I don't have to do any of 'that sort of thing' then." Jean turned and walked out, saying, "I'll go talk to Barb," as she exited the office.

She talked to Barb, who was more than happy to get the Asymetrix project back off her plate. It was therapeutic for Jean to dive back into work to get her mind away from the issues of the past few days. Exchanging emails with Donald also helped to get her back into her old routine. Like her, he'd had to field questions from too many of his coworkers about what had happened. He also had the burden of describing his arrest and night in jail. Donald also mentioned in one email that a coworker in another department requested that someone else work on their computer, as if she thought he might still be guilty.

"People suck," she wrote back to him.

She had her projects caught up and on track by 5:00 that afternoon, and she saw no reason to work any later than that. On her drive home, she heard that there had been a wreck on Highway 121, with a long backup. Normally, Donald arrived home before she did, but given the traffic report, she was not surprised when she pulled into their empty driveway. She parked in her normal spot and walked over to the front door. Their automatic garage door opener had developed a problem with the chain, and fixing it had never been a priority since they could still open the door manually. But that meant that they had developed the habit of going in through the front door.

Once she got inside, she headed for their bedroom. It was always her habit to take off her work clothes as soon as she got home, and she did so today. After using the restroom, she padded nude to the kitchen to try to come up with a dinner for her and Donald. She took a pound of hamburger meat out of the freezer and put it in the microwave, set it to defrost, and turned toward the pantry. She jumped at the sight of Donald standing by the front door in the living room.

"Oh! You startled me. I didn't hear you come in."

Donald seemed surprised. He looked at Jean in silence, turned and looked at the front door and then back at her.

"I wasn't trying to be quiet," he said.

Something about his voice sounded off. Jean stepped toward him but stopped when she saw that he was staring at her body rather than looking her in the eye.

"Is everything all right?" she asked.

He shrugged and shook his head. "Long day."

"Yeah, for me too. Why don't you come help me with dinner?"

She walked back to the pantry and took out a can of green beans and a can of stewed tomatoes. When she turned to step over to the can opener, Donald was right there next to her. Jean was so startled that she yelped and dropped the two cans, one of which almost landed on her foot.

"Donald!"

"Sorry," he said, stepping back.

Jean looked at his face, noticing that the skin was darker and more cracked than she'd ever seen it. His eyes remained fixed on her breasts, almost as if he'd never seen them before. And then the idea hit her that maybe he hadn't. She stepped away from him, backing up further into the kitchen.

"You're not Donald, are you?"

He took a step toward her and gave her a forced grin that looked nothing like Donald's natural smile. "What are you talking about?"

She was terrified, knowing what Donald's twin had done, but she kept enough wits about her to try to not let him see how scared she was. "I think you know."

He sighed and shook his head. "Was it that obvious? I mean, we both look exactly alike."

Jean thought then of the code word Agent Sloan had given them, and she wondered how to get it out without making it obvious.

"Not so exact anymore."

"What do you mean?" He took another slow step toward her as she inched closer to the back door.

"I mean you take two identical Volkswagen Beetles. One

gets stored in the garage for ten years and the other is stored out in the driveway for the same ten years. The two Volkswagens are going to look a bit different from each other after those ten years."

He shrugged, taking another step toward her.

"What do you want here?"

"I just wanted to meet my brother."

Looking past Donald's twin, she saw the front door open, and she prayed that it would be Agent Sloan coming to the rescue. She was disappointed to see Donald walk in. Before she could say anything to him, his twin had grabbed her, spun her around, and put a kitchen knife to her throat.

"Shut the fuck up," he said, and it was only then that Jean was aware that she was screaming.

33

Donald had spent the day as the company celebrity with people stopping by his desk throughout the day. A few of them, ones he didn't know well and rarely had had any interaction with, even wanted to take a selfie with him. Donald went along with it until an email went out to everyone on the Irving office distribution list telling them to leave him alone. As far as business went, it was a slow day, especially for a Monday, with Donald taking and closing just a handful of tickets. One of those tickets he took and tried to accept was reassigned to Jeff when the young lady in accounting who opened it asked to not have Donald at her desk.

"What, does she think you're guilty?" Jeff said before calling her.

Donald looked over at him and shrugged. "Who knows?" he mouthed to him as Jeff waited for the lady to answer his call.

Donald left the office right at five o'clock. On a normal day, he would beat Jean home by fifteen or twenty minutes, but he soon found himself sitting in a traffic standstill on Highway 121. He thought about calling Jean just to tell her that he would be late, but he was engrossed in a Joe Rogan podcast that was playing through his phone. He was about to pause the show and call her anyway, when traffic started moving, slowly at first, but once he got past the accident site, he was able to drive at normal speed.

As expected, Jean's Prius was in the driveway when he pulled up next to it. Donald sat in the car for a moment, thankful for a day with a sense of normalcy, even if it was a Monday. But that just meant that tomorrow was a Tuesday and would be another normal day after the insanity of the previous week.

He stepped out of his car and walked around to his front door. He and Jean had talked about leaving the front door locked at all times, so he tried it quickly and was both surprised and disappointed that it opened. What he saw inside made him forget that the door had been unlocked. Jean was in the kitchen, nude as usual, but a man dressed in a polo style shirt and trousers stood in front of her. It didn't register that the man looked exactly like himself until that man had jumped forward, grabbed Jean, spun her around, and put a knife to her throat. Jean screamed, and the man told her to shut up. Donald started to run forward, but that man screamed at him.

"Stop right there! I'll slit her throat! I swear to God!"

Donald stopped, his focus on Jean and the knife. "Don't hurt her," he said, hating that his voice sounded so weak and pleading.

"Shut the door," his double said. "And lock it."

Donald stepped back and shut the front door without taking his eyes off Jean, locking the deadbolt.

"Now, let her go," Donald said.

"Don't tell me what to do." He paused, waiting for Donald to acquiesce.

Donald exhaled. "OK," he said in as calm a voice as he could muster.

"All right. Now, we are going to sit down in the living room and have a little chat."

Donald's twin pushed Jean ahead, letting her go but keeping his hand on her bare shoulder and the point of the knife near the side of her neck. Donald's heart ached at the terror he saw in Jean's face. He was sure that her nudity made her feel even more vulnerable and helpless.

"Go," the man said to her, and she began walking toward Donald, each step slow and measured.

When they got to the sofa, the man sat her down and then

sat down beside her, keeping the point of the knife pressed against her neck. He motioned for Donald to sit on the love seat across the room from them.

"Now, here we are," the man said.

Sirens were heard in the distance.

"Why are you here?" Donald asked.

He shrugged. "I wanted to see if it was true. Did you really look just like me? And you do. It's like looking in a mirror." He glanced over at Jean. "And I got to say, keeping your woman naked all the time is just a little bit kinky, isn't it?"

"We're nudists," Donald said. "We're usually naked together. But not when we have company over."

"Am I company?"

"Uninvited company. How about I take off my shirt, and you let her put it on?"

"How about not. I like her this way."

Jean crossed her arms over her breasts as she gave Donald a look of anguish. Donald heard two cars pull right outside the house, tires squealing to a halt.

"Sounds like you have more company," the man said.

"Your name is Randy, right," Donald said.

The man shrugged. "I guess so, but I haven't gone by that name in a few years."

A cell phone rang, the sound echoing from the kitchen.

"That's my phone," Jean said.

Randy pushed her up, stood up himself, and returned the knife to her throat.

"Go get it," he said to Donald.

Donald rose and walked into the kitchen. Randy angled himself and Jean so that he could see Donald every step of the way. Jean's phone was on the counter next to the stove. The screen was lit up as it rang, moving slightly from the vibration. Donald picked it up and answered the call.

"Hello."

"Hello, this is Special Agent Jeremy Sloan of the FBI. Who is this please?"

"Hi, Agent Sloan. This is Donald White."

"Is everyone in the house unharmed?"

"Yeah, so far."

Seeing Randy motion him back to the living room, Donald

started walking that way.

"I take it Randall Jacob Crum is in the house with you."

"Yes. He's currently holding a knife to my wife's neck."

"Can you switch the phone to speaker?"

Donald meant to walk as close to Jean as he could, but Randy was backing up with her. He motioned to the love seat with the knife, and Donald walked that way. He switched the phone to speaker and set it on the coffee table in the middle of the room.

"OK, Agent Sloan, you're on speaker."

Donald sat back down on the love seat, and Randy returned to the sofa with Jean.

"Mr. Crum. This is Special Agent Jeremy Sloan from the Federal Bureau of Investigation."

"How are you doing, Special Agent Jeremy Sloan?"

Donald heard the click of the back yard gate on the side of the house. He watched Randy, but he didn't react to it. Hopefully, he hadn't heard it.

"I'll be better once we get a resolution to the situation we're in. Why don't you step outside onto the front lawn so we can resolve this peacefully?"

"I'm not quite ready to do that."

"How do we get you ready to do that without any harm to Mr. or Mrs. White?"

"That's the trick, isn't it?"

"Can Mrs. White talk?"

"Yes," Jean said. "I'm here."

"You OK?"

"I've been better."

"I know. I apologize. I should have had someone here before you got home."

"You're here now."

"That's enough of that," Randy said, pressing the knife blade closer to her neck.

Donald started to get up, but Randy pushed Jean toward the end of the sofa and pulled a gun out of his pants pocket with his now free hand and pointed at him.

"What is it that you want?" Sloan's voice said over the phone speaker.

Randy extended the hand with the knife back toward Jean,

and for an instant, Donald thought he was moving to stab her. When Crum's arm stopped, holding the knife about an inch from Jean's neck, Donald exhaled. He hadn't even realized he had been holding his breath.

"I don't know," Randy said. "I guess I just want to know what life could have been like if…". His voice trailed off.

Donald saw Jean's eyes darting around the room. She was on the edge of the sofa near the end table, the one with the marble sculpture of Athena that her grandmother had made. When her eyes locked with Donald's, he subtty shook his head at her.

"What I can promise you," Agent Sloan said, "is that your life will be very different after today. You'll be taken care of. Roof over your head, three meals a day, medical care. Everything. For the rest of your life."

"Until someone sticks a needle in my arm in the death chamber."

"Is that what it's going to take to resolve this peacefully? To take the death penalty off the table?"

"Can you do that?"

"I can't, but I can talk to the District Attorney who can. But even he can't speak for the jurisdictions in other states."

"What other states?"

Sloan snorted in derision. "Don't insult my intelligence. Your DNA profile is connected to cases in multiple states."

"My DNA profile is the same as Mr. White's here. How do you know it wasn't him."

"We didn't at first. A thorough investigation proved otherwise. That same investigation pointed to you."

"He has a gun," Donald said.

"We know. We can see into the house."

Randy looked around at the windows and the small glass area high up on the front door. As he did so, he lowered the knife. Jean moved like lightning, leaning away from Randy, grabbing the sculpture, and swinging it at him with both hands. The knife came back up as the marble Athena slammed into the side of his head. Donald leapt up from the love seat to help Jean. Randy pulled the trigger of the gun in his left hand, the crack of the shot deafening. Donald felt a sting in his shoulder, but he still rushed forward and slammed into Randy, grabbing the wrist with the knife and pulling it away from Jean.

The door burst open as Donald twisted Randy to the floor. He was too close for Randy to get the gun pointed at him, but he still got off another shot that seemed to hit the ceiling. The jolt of hitting the floor knocked the gun out of Randy's hand. Donald dropped a knee into Randy's neck. Randy gagged. His hand unclenched, and he dropped the knife to the floor beside him. Donald was powerfully pulled from Randy and thrown to the floor, and two other men dropped onto Randy. Donald's hands were held onto the floor. Jean rushed to his side between the men who had pulled him off Randy.

"Let him go," she said. "He's the good guy."

"Step back ma'am," one of them said.

Donald could see Agent Sloan pulling Jean away, talking softly to her. "Let's get you dressed," he heard Sloan say.

He turned his head as Agent Sloan led her away, trying to track where they went. That was when he felt the blood on his shirt and the pain in his shoulder.

<h1 style="text-align:center">34</h1>

Sloan had to practically drag Jean away from Donald when she saw that he had been shot. She might not care that she was naked in front of fifty police officers and investigators, but she might regret it afterward. He got her into their bedroom and left her alone to get dressed. He walked back into the living room to see two identical men. One was in handcuffs and had been hauled to his feet, blood running down the side of his head. The other had a bullet wound to the shoulder and was being attended to by two paramedics. Jean emerged from her bedroom mere seconds after he'd left her, in shorts and a t-shirt but still barefoot.

The paramedics had cut Donald's shirt off of him and were looking at his right shoulder. To Sloan, it looked like the bullet had gone through his trapezius muscle just above the clavicle. A few inches to the left, it would have gone through his neck and killed him.

Jean tried to get to to Donald, but the paramedics were still working all around him.

"He's going to be all right ma'am," one of the paramedics said.

"Jean, look at me," Sloan said.

Jean stood and faced him. He put his hand on her chin and raised it.

"You have a cut on your neck."

"He pressed that knife into me pretty hard. Thankfully, we

haven't sharpened our knives in a long time."

Sloan turned to two paramedics who had just walked in. "Can we get some antiseptic for her neck?"

"Sure," one of them said.

One of the paramedics took Jean outside toward the ambulance and out of the way of the guys working on Donald. The fourth paramedic began working on Crum's head wound. Sloan walked up to Crum and took pleasure in what he was about to say.

"Randall Jacob Crum, you are under arrest for the murders of Marcella Aguilar, Elena Robles, Patricia Garcia, and several others." He would list his rights when he had him in an interrogation room.

Crum just looked at him with a dullness in his eyes.

"He may need stitches," the paramedic said.

"Can you do that here? I don't want him in a civilian hospital."

"Sure thing."

Sloan found a Lewisville Police Department Sergeant. "I want several officers with him when the paramedic sutures his head wound."

"Yes sir."

He followed the group leading Crum outside to the ambulance, motioning to one of the crime scene lab guys as he walked.

"I want samples taken from under his fingernails," he told him.

"What am I looking for?"

"Blood or skin cells that can be matched to any of the victims, probably the most recent."

"Will do."

"And after that, do the same thing with Donald White. Preferably before he's transported to the hospital. And make sure the samples are well marked. Don't use their names. Mark one 'Head Wound' and the other 'Shoulder Wound' just to show we aren't assuming anything."

"Sure thing."

Sloan watched the lab tech head into the ambulance with Crum and the paramedics. The entire block had been cordoned off, and he could see news vans from all the network affiliates just beyond the barricade. Even though he had officially been removed from the case earlier in the day, the arrest was still his as a result of his surveillance of the Whites' house. So he was going to take the credit for it while also reassuring the public that one of the most dangerous killers the area had ever seen was safely in custody.

As the crime scene investigation went on throughout the night, Crum's car was found three blocks over from the White residence. Inside the car were a bunch of clothes, a few little trinkets, and a wooden box containing thirty-three patches of human skin, all but two of them with tattoos. The gun that Crum had shot Donald White with was a Ruger LCP 380 Automatic registered to Mindy Gutierrez, a murder victim from Needles, California three years before. Donald White was taken by ambulance to Parkland Hospital. Jean rode with him, but Sloan was able to get a statement from her before she left. She told him that she had thought Crum was Donald White at first but that she realized he wasn't just before White himself walked in the door.

"So you're sure the man we have in custody now is not your husband?" Sloan had asked her.

"I'm positive."

"Good," he said. That made him feel easier as Sloan himself couldn't tell the two men apart. He figured that a woman who had been married to one of them as long as Jean had *could* tell them apart.

Despite having gone without sleep for over 24 hours now, Sloan still went to Lew Sterrett to conduct the first interview with Randall Jacob Crum, taking Sam Blackman with him. When they got to the jail, Crum was ushered in from his holding cell. There was a large bandage on the side of his head. He sat down at the table across from Sloan and Blackman. Sloan read him his Miranda rights.

"With these rights in mind, are you willing to talk with us?" Sloan asked.

"I got nothing to say. My name is Donald White. Whoever you're calling Randall Jacob Crum is still out there with my wife."

"Is that so?"

"Yes."

"Then how is it that you shot Donald White?"

"I'm Donald White."

"How is it that you shot your twin brother? That gun was registered to Mindy Gutierrez who was found murdered in the desert outside Needles two years ago last March. Donald White couldn't have had that gun."

"I took it from Crum when we were in the house together."

"Horseshit. We heard and saw everything that was going on in that house."

"How could you see? No one was in there with us."

"Thermal imaging. It was you who had the knife to Jean White's throat, you who had the gun pointed at Donald White."

"I'm Donald White."

Sloan sat back, glanced at Sam Blackman then looked back at Crum. "Are you serious? That's going to be your bullshit story?"

Crum shrugged. "That's the truth. Now, I could get a lawyer and talk to him about it."

"That's your right, but I don't think you want to do that."

Sloan sat in silence after this, staring at Crum. He was running on the pure adrenaline from finally having The Tattoo Collector in custody and sitting in front of him. Sloan had zero doubt of that. But he knew that when that adrenaline kick subsided, he'd crash from exhaustion and sleep deprivation. Crum sat staring back at him with a blank look on his face.

"Why did you kill Marcella Aguilar?" Sloan asked when Crum finally looked down.

"Who?"

"Marcella Aguilar. My girlfriend's roommate. Were you trying to send me a message?"

Crum shook his head. "I didn't kill anyone."

Sloan sat and stared back at him in silence again, betting that a narcissist like Crum couldn't bear to see anyone else given credit for what he had done. Crum stared back at him just like before. Sam Blackman sat beside Sloan, impassively looking at his notes.

"I would imagine," Crum finally said after several minutes, "that Crum saw this person…"

"Marcella Aguilar," Sloan prompted.

"Marcella, and he just had to have her."

Sloan saw Blackman jot something on his notepad, not that it mattered that much since the whole interrogation was being recorded on video and audio.

"He did?" Sloan said.

"Yeah. I mean, that's the way I imagine it happened."

Sloan and Blackman looked at each other and smiled. Crum couldn't help but talk about himself. It might take a few hours or a few days, but Sloan now knew exactly how this would turn out.

<h1 align="center">35</h1>

Jean and Donald both spent a week away from work. Donald was kept one night in the hospital before they let him go home. The bullet had gone through the trapezoid muscle in his shoulder but miraculously missed any bones. His right arm would be in a sling for a couple of weeks just to keep the shoulder immobilized so it could heal.

Jean supposed that the nightmares that had plagued Donald for the past few years would stop now. They only ever came once every few weeks anyway, so it would be difficult to tell for sure. But Jean was having nightmares herself, ones in which it was Donald who was in jail and his twin brother living with her, pretending to be him. She knew that was impossible. She had grilled Donald incessantly about their past vacations and experiences, making sure that he knew so many things that his twin could never have learned. But still, the nightmares persisted.

She and Donald returned to work the same day, a Monday exactly one week after the arrest of Randall Jacob Crum. Agent Sloan called Jean's cell that day asking if he could stop by their house that evening. She agreed and then sent an email to Donald telling him to stay dressed when he got home as Agent Sloan would be visiting. Other than that, her day proceeded normally. She and Donald had exchanged emails throughout the day as they always did, with Donald commenting that it was strange being back into their regular routine after all that had happened. But he didn't comment on how the others were treating him. During her absence, her Asymetrix project had been, once again, reassigned to Barb who after a week had put so much work into it that Jean didn't try to get it back.

Agent Sloan rang her doorbell less than two minutes after she arrived home.

"Come on in," she said. "Donald's in the bathroom, but he should be out in a minute."

"Thank you." He looked at the door frame. "I see you got this fixed."

"Yeah, we had that done the day after."

"Sorry for bashing it in. If you still have the receipt, why don't you give it to me, and I'll see if I can get the Bureau to reimburse you."

"That would be great."

He came in, and Jean motioned to the sofa. "Would you like something to drink?"

"No, I'm fine," he said, taking his seat on the end of the sofa.

He looked at the end table. The sculpture of Athena was missing, taken as evidence. Sloan had told her that she would get it back once the case had been adjudicated.

"It's strange, being here again," he said. "The two biggest arrests of my career happened here. One in error, one not."

Jean sat on the love seat opposite him. Donald appeared, his right arm in the sling. Agent Sloan hopped up and the two men shared a lefty handshake.

"Donald, how are you?"

"I'm good. How are you?"

"Fine."

Sloan retook his seat, and Donald sat next to Jean.

"I wanted to come by and tell you a little more about the case. This is all confidential, of course, so don't share it with anyone."

"OK," Donald said.

"Right from the get-go, Crum started off claiming to be you, and that you were Crum."

Donald put his hand on Jean's leg. "Nonsense," he said.

"That's what I told him. But still, he couldn't stop talking about himself, just in hypothetical terms. During the arrest, we took samples from under his fingernails. We did the same with you."

"Oh. That's what that was about."

"Yeah. When we got the results back, yours were clean. His contained trace amounts of DNA from Marcella Aguilar, his final victim. So we confronted him with this evidence once it got back to us. He finally started talking then. So far, he's confessed to forty-eight murders, including that of his mother. Your birth mother."

The room was silent for a moment. Jean grabbed Donald's hand and held it tightly.

"I figured he killed our birth mother when I heard what had happened to her," Donald finally said.

"Forty-eight," Jean said in a solemn voice.

Sloan shrugged. "Is the number really forty-eight? Who knows. Now that he's in custody, he knows he'll never be let out. He may be inflating that number just to cement his fame. Or infamy, however you want to look at it. We do have evidence that he committed at least thirty-three murders besides that of his mother."

"The tattoos?" Donald said.

Sloan looked at him and nodded. After a pause, he said, "Well, that's it. That's all I came to say."

"Thank you," Jean said.

"Oh, and I want to apologize again. For both your arrest and for not being back here when you got home from work last week. Another thing Crum said was that he got into your house the night before, while you were sleeping."

"Oh my God," Jean said, not meaning for it to be aloud.

"He knew we were watching your house, so he came from the back, entering the yard of the neighbor behind you, jumping the fence, and then picking the lock on your back door. I've scanned the audio recordings from that night, but I can't find anything that the microphones picked up. He was very quiet."

"So he could have killed us in our sleep," Donald said.

"He could have. But I think he just had to experience a little bit of what your life was like. He's what we call a narcissistic sociopath, so having someone who was virtually identical to himself threw him for a loop."

"Maybe we should have let you put cameras in," Donald

said.

Sloan shrugged. "It's all hindsight now."

"Well, you called it," Donald said. "You knew he'd come here."

"I thought he would, yeah."

They all sat in silence for a moment before Donald spoke.

"One thing really bothers me."

"What's that?" Sloan said.

"If our circumstances were reversed, if I were the one in the NICU, the one our birth mother had kept, and Randy had been the one given up for adoption, would I have been pushed into becoming what he became? I mean, we are identical. The only thing that's different is how we were raised. If I had been raised by the people who raised him… How do I know there's not a monster lurking inside me?"

"I've told you before, you're nothing like him," Jean said.

Sloan looked at them. "Killers like Randall Jacob Crum are rare, thank God. Lots of people are raised just like he was and don't become sociopathic. From what I know about you and how you see the world, I don't think you would have succumbed the way he did."

"But there's no way to tell for sure."

"No, there's not. But take solace in who you are now. You can't ask hypothetical questions that you will never have an answer to." He took his phone from his jacket pocket, looked at the time displayed on the screen, and stood up. "I have to go. FBI work is never done."

Jean stepped forward and hugged him. "Thank you."

Donald shook his hand. "I'm glad it was you who arrested me. That sounds strange, doesn't it?"

Sloan laughed. "Not at all. I take it as a compliment." He stepped toward the door and allowed Jean to open it for him. "You two have a good night."

www.ingramcontent.com/pod-product-compliance
Lightning Source LLC
Chambersburg PA
CBHW061209210726
48294CB00006B/1805